ALL THE PIECES COMING TOGETHER

collected works

SONORA TAYLOR

MANTA·PRESS

To everyone who's helped me and supported me.

TABLE OF CONTENTS

*A full list of content warnings can be found on page 232

FOREWORD

by Steve Stred

Let me tell you about a song from an album by a musician you've probably never heard or heard of.

Go to YouTube on your phone or computer—I'll wait while you do this—and search "Road to Hattiesburg" by Robert Earl Reed. It's from his 2011 album *Carlene*. It's four minutes and one second long, and it's a song that I've never forgotten since I first heard it. It's from an album filled with folk-Americana songs that have a cadence, a timbre, and a resonance that vibrate through you when you listen to it.

So, what does that have to do with the book you're holding?

Well, how that song makes you feel is the same as how reading Sonora Taylor will affect you.

Back in 2019, I was a part of the Kendall Reviews review team, and a novel was offered for us to read titled *Without Condition*. It was from a new-to-me author, but I was intrigued. I wasn't sure what to expect based off the synopsis and cover, but what I read has never left my brain.

Reading that novel not only introduced me to a writer who constantly challenges me as a reader but also led to us developing a wonderful friendship. We've read and supported each other's works, offered blurbs for one another, and Sonora kindly wrote the foreword to my *Father of Lies: The Complete Series* omnibus when it was released.

No matter whether Sonora is writing short fiction or through to novel length, you're sure to find that her work contains layers, heart, and a willingness to unnerve the reader in every sense of the word.

A perfect example of what Sonora creates is the story "Weary Bones," which was featured in her 2019 collection *Little Paranoias: Stories*. And to understand the creepy, dread-infused style of storytelling, one needs to look no further than her 2020 novella *Seeing Things*.

Time and time again, Sonora does a pristine job of dangling the carrot out in front for the reader to follow, only to discover that the carrot is rotting and covered in squirming maggots.

Over the last number of years, she's churned out novellas such as *Errant Roots* and released the short story collections *Someone to Share My Nightmares* and *Recreational Panic: Stories*. And she still found time to edit *Diet Riot: A Fatterpunk Anthology* with Nico Bell. Sonora is busy, busting ass and constantly working to write and release fiction that whole-heartedly crushes the reader.

All of that led me to initially reach out to her regarding this collection you hold in your hands. For a very brief time, I flirted with the idea of publishing people through my own small press. Sonora was one of the first people I invited, and I couldn't wait to get this out in the wider world. Sadly, things on my end changed, but I knew Sonora's book would find a home and find one quick, and to see it with Tim and the fine folks at Manta Press has me over the moon.

Within these pages, you'll find some of Sonora's favorite stories, some new stuff and, of course, you'll find the thing that highlights her work and makes her a "must-read" author: her prose and writing voice.

Much like what I said about Robert Earl Reed applies to Sonora's writing. There's a resonance to it. A timbre and a cadence that speak to the heart of the observation she's detailing and the lives that the reader has found themselves involved within. Her stories showcase Americana and the roots of the day-to-day, but all with a Taylor twist.

For long-time Sonora fans, you'll know what you're about to experience.

For new readers, prepare yourself.

These stories are bits of your day that'll get under your skin and before you know it, you've become that dangling carrot with squirming maggots just below the surface.

Enjoy,

Steve Stred
Edmonton, Alberta

Author's Introduction

I still remember when the concept for a story dug its way into my mind and wouldn't let go. I was walking home from work, passing by the houses between the Metro station and my old apartment. I was imagining stories in my mind, as I often did, and had never stopped doing even though I hadn't actually finished anything in years. A thought came to me that made me laugh: what if a serial killer found a place so perfect to hide the bodies, that there was no one around to hide?

From that thought came "All the Pieces Coming Together," the first story I started and finished in over ten years (the last being a vampire story I wrote in college and probably won't publish). From that story came four novels, five collections, and numerous short stories written and published between 2016 and 2025.

Most of those stories came from the same process, where I laughed at or was horrified by turning something mundane into something sinister. "The Crow's Gift," the story I wrote after "All the Pieces Coming Together," came from a sweet article about crows bringing trinkets to a neighborhood girl who fed them. I wondered what else a crow, famous for its ability to hold grudges, would be willing to do for someone who was wronged. "Stick Figure Family," one of my most popular pieces, gives a new meaning to what those stick figure children we see all over back windshields actually signify. My newest story that ends this collection, "The Ashiest Place Unearthed," was inspired by how many people secretly scatter the ashes of their loved ones in theme parks. What if there was a darker secret motivating those people?

There were other inspirations, of course. Three stories were inspired by prompts for anthologies. One of these, "Hearts Are Just 'Likes,'" became the first story I sold, appearing in the contemporary Poe anthology *Quoth the Raven* (Camden Park Press, ed. Lyn Worthen). Some stories, like "Someone to Share My Nightmares," started as something very different before becoming what you see in this book. (For that story, I originally envisioned a novel about a film professor following her obsession with a filmmaker to her detriment, one I may still write.)

The following omnibus brings together stories from my first four collections, a story originally published in 2018, and two new ones. With the exception of "Shell," I've arranged them in chronological order based on when their collections were published. While it was tempting to go back and edit the older stories, I decided not to pull a George Lucas on these pieces and leave them as they were originally published. In addition to still being proud of these works, I wanted to show how my writing has grown and changed from 2016 to today—as well as what remains distinctly the same. You'll see several themes reoccur: serial killers, nature's revenge on humanity, ghosts, and above all, anxiety.

I hope you enjoy this journey into my writing from the past several years. Watch your step—you never know what's just around the corner. Or what's behind you. Or worse, what's deep within you.

Sonora Taylor
April 15, 2025

ALL THE PIECES COMING TOGETHER

The branches whip in the wind as the sky bruises and bleeds into night. A lone bird chirps, desperately seeking a mate, but the only call back is the rustle of pine needles that cling to their branches. There is not a human soul for miles.

It's the perfect place to hide a body. The trouble is, there isn't anybody to hide.

I'm a serial killer — or at least, I would be if there were anyone around to kill. I picked an amazing spot to begin my life of murderous solitude. I soon realized it was a little too solitary, though, so my career has largely been dicking around online (when I can get a connection) and watching movies.

I've had some practice, of course. I began where we almost all begin: helpless animals. They were easy to start with because many people didn't think twice about them. "Oh, don't mind him, he's just a boy — boys sometimes hurt animals." Normal boys sometimes squash bugs or kick the family pet. A normal boy doesn't dismember dogs and bury each piece in a different part of the woods that, if unearthed, would spell their name in binary code.

It's a good thing I started with animals, because that's all I've got out here. I even tried to get as creative as I would with a person. Unfortunately, the deer just can't pick up on the patterns. I worked really hard to shape their limbs into that peace sign, and what did they do? Nothing. Ungrateful bastards.

Further, there are too many deer for their absence to make much difference. People are limited, which makes their disposal all the more rewarding. Their disappearance leads to a crisis, which leads to a puzzle, one that I've created and know they'll never solve. People are limited. People are missed.

I miss them.

I want to be near them again. We all want closeness and companionship. Some of us just gain that by burying people in the floorboards. The floorboards of my lonely cabin, in these lonely woods, where no one can find them – and where I can't find anyone.

I need to get out of the woods and find some people.

First, I need to find a place to go.

Fortunately, my Internet is working, perhaps suggesting that tonight is my night. I look at what's around here. Not much of anything, naturally. There are schools further out, but it's late and most students will have walked home alone by now. There are churches, but I don't trust anyone in church on a Tuesday.

Ah, here we go – a bar, called The Best Shot. Fitting, as it's my best chance at finding someone tonight. It's about an hour away, though I could probably speed most of the way without fail. There aren't any cops out here either.

I quickly make myself presentable. I shave the scant beard I've grown and run a comb through my short brown hair. Before moving here, I was a man who'd charmed quite a few panties into my palm. I was ready to turn that charm back on, albeit for a much different purpose.

I hop in my piece-of-shit car and drive down the highway. It's a pretty night — lots of stars, a cool breeze. It is insanely dark. It's the kind that can almost make you feel enclosed by its opacity. My first couple nights sleeping out here, I almost had panic attacks. I couldn't see my own hands in front of my face. What if I could never see again? What if darkness was all I had left? At least in death, you're unaware of the darkness surrounding you. It's a courtesy I hope to extend to others.

The road drags on endlessly, even as I speed. Fortunately, no deer are slowing me down. Maybe my artwork is working well enough to deter them from running in front of my car.

Slowly the darkness opens into streetlamps and a Wal-Mart. It's always the first sign of civilization when you leave the middle of nowhere. The lone Wal-Mart gives way to occasional gas stations, ones so isolated that I'm sure you could see Jason Voorhees pumping gas and not think twice. The gas stations become strip malls, and the strip malls become chain restaurants.

Finally, tucked between some pine trees just past a Lowes, I see it — The Best Shot. I'm relieved to see some cars parked out front. I'd worried slightly that even if there were people around, they'd be choosing to smoke meth in the privacy of their own garden sheds instead of getting drunk in a bar.

I walk inside, and it looks like every stereotype of a podunk bar you'd come to expect: one of the nation's last surviving jukeboxes, an assortment of old men and hard women, and a bartender who probably got a few of her tats in prison. The scent of vodka and beer hangs in the air, and it looks like the kind of place that would've smelled of cigarettes if it weren't against the law to smoke inside. This is one law I'm thankful for. An asthma attack is the last thing I need when scouting potential victims.

I move towards the bar, some money in my pocket. I came prepared for a couple of beers — enough to seem loose (and loosen up) while staying sober enough to drive someone back to the middle of nowhere. I'm not going to be driven home by someone and then kill them in their own house. I'm perfectly able to host a murder, thank you.

I take a seat, and the bartender comes over with a look on her face that tells me she'd rather be anywhere than here. "What'll it be, hon," she says as a statement, not a question. Age and – from the sound of it – smoking since kindergarten have not been kind to her.

"Just a Bud, please." Do people still drink Bud? I keep reading about craft beer online. I doubt this place even knows what craft beer is.

She wordlessly pours my Bud, one of two tap handles (confirming my craft beer suspicions), and places it in front of me.

"Keeping it simple, huh?"

I stop mid-sip and look in the direction of the voice. I see a woman I hadn't noticed previously. She's suspiciously hot in these surroundings. Auburn hair in a ponytail, rimless glasses, tits peeking out over a pink bustier. She's drinking what looks like a whiskey sour, dunking the maraschino cherry up and down in the ice. The effect causes a ripple in her breasts, one I try very hard not to stare at.

"Simple?" I ask. Well, stammer. I am a cool and collected killer, but I am also a warm-blooded man, one who hasn't even seen a woman in a very long time.

"'Just a Bud, please.'" Her imitation man voice makes her sound even sexier. Jesus, I hadn't accounted for being turned on. "You're just going to ask for that? You're not going to see what else they have to offer?"

I sip my beer to try and quell my ever-growing boner, and say calmly, coolly, "Well, forgive me for assuming that this place doesn't have much creativity to offer."

She has a small and wispy laugh that disappears like a puff of smoke. Her eyes reconnect with mine, and she says, "Sometimes all you have to do is ask." Her eyes don't leave mine as she slowly bites one of the cherries and sucks it off the stem.

That's it. Killing is 50/50, but I'm definitely fucking tonight.

I scooch one barstool over so that I'm next to her. She doesn't move, much to my delight, and we start the small talk that precludes fucking. I tell her my name, that I work in lumber and live out near the woods. It's lonely, but it pays the bills. I'm hopeful that sympathy works in my sexual favor — as does buying the next round, which I do at this point.

Her name is Candace, and she's a nurse. She's off tonight, and she figured she'd stop in for a drink or two, have a little fun, maybe find a little trouble. Our knees have moved toward each other at this point, so she has no problem dropping her finger on my wrist when she says this.

I stare at her finger with its perfect pink tip. I imagine it disconnected from her bangled wrist, floating over my own. Each piece of her starts to detach from itself, floating in various places in my mind. The human body is nothing but fragments, held together by sinew and bone; and I can take it apart, piece-by-piece. I can reassemble as I wish or scatter the pieces to points of no return. It's a control I crave, one that, combined with the sexual longing an average person would be feeling right now, begins to consume me. I can feel my dick stiffening against my pants, my pulse raising rapidly.

It's the pulse that Candace notices first. She places more fingers on my wrist, turning it over. I let her. Giving her some control now will make it easier to completely master her later. I already imagine her hands on my face, her legs on my bed, her breasts on my mantle. I can't wait any longer.

"All I have to do is ask, right?"

She returns her gaze to me and gives me a sly smile. "Depends on the question."

I take a final gulp of beer. "Do you want to get out of here?"

Everything is going according to plan. Well, it will once we stop making out.

We haven't even left the parking lot of The Best Shot. One minute I'm all set to drive her to the cabin, and then she brushed my hair before I could open the passenger-side door, and I couldn't help myself and we started kissing against the car. No, kissing's too demure a way to describe it. The only thing keeping us from getting arrested is the fact that we have our clothes on.

I'm not one of those killers who's afraid of sex or women or can only do it on top of a corpse or in a bathtub full of someone's blood or something. I love sex. Another disadvantage of my chosen locale. I really didn't think that one through. And now, I risk letting my hormones get the better of me and precluding Candace from reaching her final destination.

"We've gotta get to my place," I manage to croak out. She continues kissing my neck while I speak, and I can feel her breasts brushing against my shoulder.

"Okay," is all she manages to say. I've moved to her shoulder, and we move back to each other's mouths. I run my hands up and down her sides and she grabs my ass, grinding against me. Surely, she can feel my erection. I contemplate just doing it on the hood of the car.

"The sooner we get home," I say, pulling myself away again, "the sooner we can do this right."

This stops us both. She turns back to face the car, and I open the door before I have a chance to change my mind and start taking her from behind. She's barely in before I slam the door shut, rush to the driver's side, and peel out of the parking lot, heading home for an evening of sex and murder. My heart — not to mention my prick — can barely stand it.

The road is even emptier than when I made my way out here earlier. Candace rolls down the window and lets her fingers float in the breeze, arching her back ever-so-slightly against the seat and letting out a delicate moan of pleasure. She's pleasing herself, playing with me, or maybe a little of both. I try to keep my eyes ahead of me. The last thing I want is a car wreck to rob me of this kill.

"You really do live far away," she says after we've been driving for some time, when the strip malls have become the lone Wal-Mart but have not yet become trees again.

"I like to be near the source of my work," I say. This in itself isn't necessarily a lie.

"I kind of like it," she replies. "Seems peaceful."

I sigh, thinking of how long it's been since I've had sex, and of all the dead deer. "Sometimes it's too peaceful."

I feel her hand slink down onto my leg, and hear her seatbelt unbuckle. She moves closer to me, and I pray she isn't contemplating road head —it would be amazing, but I really need to be able to drive.

Her head stays above my pants, though, and rests on my shoulder. She whispers, "It won't be tonight." And then she bites my ear.

I speed up substantially. We have to get home.

In my chosen line of work, it helps to be handsome. Drawing people in is part of the battle. People have to trust you if you're going to successfully kill them. A great way to get people to trust you is to get them to want to fuck you. And a great way to get them to want to fuck you is to be handsome. Which, fortunately, I am. At least that's what I tell myself. Otherwise, the fact that my potential victim has gone from straddling a barstool to straddling my lap in roughly three hours just seems a little too easy.

We've made it to the house — well, to my driveway. We have yet to get out of the car. As soon as I put the car in park, we started making out again. Candace's jacket is in the backseat, but otherwise, we stay clothed. This hasn't stopped me from rubbing her through her panties, or her from grinding on my cock.

"Let's go inside," she finally breathes. I almost don't hear her, as I'm focused entirely on her body. Seduction was a tactic I had in mind, but this is bordering on madness. I cannot stop touching her, nor her me. I try to cool myself off by thinking of the after party, of carving her up and spreading the pieces, but this only makes it worse. It gives me a secret, one she'll never know until it's too late. And here she is, giving herself to me. It's too delicious to bear.

And giving herself she is — in full. We make it into the house, finally, but only to the couch. She drops her giant purse on the floor, a loud thwack echoing across the floorboards as she quickly sheds pieces of clothing: glasses, jewelry, skirt. My shirt and belt follow suit, until I'm down to my briefs and she's annoyingly clad in her underwear and bustier.

I grab at her top and she takes my hands, showing the first sign of resistance all night. She pushes my hands away, holding them firmly on the couch.

"What are you …" I start to say, praying she isn't stopping things here. I also start to contemplate a much sooner death for her than I anticipated.

But she interrupts me, placing one hand over my lips. I forget my frustration and start biting her thumb. She takes it back and slowly unfastens her bustier from the back. It's the slowest thing she's done all night, and it's worth it.

The moment her breasts spill into view, things become an immediate blur. I'm aware of launching myself into them, kissing and biting with abandon while she holds my head close and groans with pleasure. Soon we're standing up, because a couch is a fine place for fucking, but not nearly as good as a bed. Hell, it's not even as good as a kitchen table, where we make a pit stop so I can pull down her panties and start eating her out.

I am aware, as we stand back up and continue on to the bedroom, that my plans have gone somewhat off course. I'd forgotten how hard it is to stay focused when a hot naked woman is present. But for the time being, as we roll around over my old comforter, I don't care. Her time will come. For now, I'll happily kiss and bite various places on her skin, groan while she scratches my back, and thrust my cock inside of her from various positions.

I could fuck her all night and probably most of the next, but I'm only able to come so much. I lay next to her, regrettably spent, as she is still able to cuddle on me and nibble my earlobe. Women will never know how lucky they are to be able to keep going after they come. Hell, at least with Candace, coming seems to make her want more.

She slows when she sees that, for me at least, the fucking is finished. "Where's your bathroom?" she asks. I merely point, still out of breath. I pray this is the only indication I might have given her of how long it's been since I've had sex. I watch her as she walks, naked, to the living room to grab her purse and then shuts herself in the bathroom. I hear her loudly pee.

Okay, maybe now I can begin to focus. What next? I recall my various hiding places for assorted weapons and drugs. None of them are immediately under the bed. I could go looking for them while she's in the bathroom. Then I hear her flush and abandon that idea. The door stays closed, and I hear her rummaging through her purse, brushing her hair. Time is slipping away.

Stay the night — she'll probably stay the night. I did drive her here, after all. I'm her ride home. *In more ways than one.* I smile and feel myself stiffen again. She'll fall asleep, breathing lightly next to me, and then …

I'm broken from my glimpse in the future by the sound of the bathroom door opening. I look forward and she's back — hair brushed, fresh coat of lipstick, still naked. Her purse is in her hand. Her eyes fall on my newly awakened cock, and she smiles. "Not completely spent, huh?" she says, moving towards me.

I don't want to make her promises I can't keep, but it's hard to speak as she drops her purse on the bedside table and straddles over me. "I - I guess not …" I manage to say, before I'm silenced by her mouth.

Okay, no falling asleep yet. I'll deal. I run my hands over her ass, kissing her, keeping it slow. She grinds on top of me while her hands run all over my body. Well, her hand. Where's her other hand?

She pulls away, and I realize three things — both my legs and one arm are pinned under her surprisingly-strong legs, one hand is pinning my free arm down, and her other hand is pressing a rag into my face. It smells off. Oh fuck, oh fuck, OH FU -

Thankfully I wake up. I'm still naked and still in bed. Now I'm tightly secured to the bedposts by my wrists and ankles. The room gradually comes into focus. I don't see Candace. Where did she go?

I can't believe this. I knew it was too easy. I never should have let her take control like that. God, letting her get on top? Yes, hindsight is 20/20. But you need to be more aware. Victims don't fall into your lap, and Candace isn't a victim, not by a long shot.

Candace isn't even here. Where the fuck is she? Did she just decide to tie me up and peace out? Maybe she took the car. Well, I won't exactly miss it. But these binds are pretty strong — they'll take hours to get out of if I'm here alone.

I hear her footsteps, dashing that theory aside. Then what? I don't suppose she's secretly into BDSM and this is just a precursor to more sex.

My vision is almost completely focused and restores itself just in time to see her walk into the room. She's no longer naked, but wearing purple nursing scrubs, just unfastened enough to show her cleavage. Where did she get those from? I notice her purse in her gloved hands. It's huge — probably big enough for the scrubs. And the rag. What else?

"Oh good," she says, stopping next to the bed. She rubs her hand through my hair. What had been a major turn-on now sends a sickening chill down my neck. My toes curl and my heart rate quickens. "You're awake."

"What the fuck is going on?" I ask. She gets on top of me again. It's amazing how that suddenly feels old and unwelcome. "What the fuck did you do to me?"

"Just put you to sleep for a little bit," she replies, tracing her fingers over my chest.

"Put me to sleep?" I snort in disgust. "You knocked me out, you fucking bitch. Why did you tie me up?" I give her a coy look, one final bit of hope. "If you were into this, you could've just asked."

She laughs. It's a little sexy, but mostly ugly. I do the worst thing any potential serial killer could do: I get scared. I don't like the way she's touching me, especially as her fingers near my throat. I start panicking, thinking she must know who I am, what I am, and plans to stop it. To stop me.

"Look," I say, just wanting my own freedom at this point. "Whatever you think, it's … Just let me go. I'll drive you back, and we can go our separate ways. I won't hurt you, I promise, I —"

A flash of genuine confusion crossing her face before it disappears and settles into smug control. "Hurt me?" She leers. "You can't."

"And I won't," I continue. "I don't know what you thought, why you wanted to tie me up, what you know or think or figured out …" Her face stays stoic, though I can see her thoughts racing. "But whatever it is, I won't do it. Not now."

"Do what?" she asks.

I mentally kick myself for panicking. I sigh, resigning myself to just telling the truth. "I won't … you know, kill you."

She stares at me blankly for a few long moments. Then she cocks her head, keeping eye contact with me as she straightens her posture. Her hands leave my chest.

"I didn't tie you up because I thought you were going to kill me," she says at last. I quietly sigh and simultaneously feel my heart sink.

I notice that one hand is reaching into her purse. My pulse races as she withdraws a single, sharp scalpel.

"I tied you up," she says, looking me dead in the eyes, "because I'm going to kill you."

You've got to be shitting me.

I stare at her. I'm not even scared. I'm fucking pissed. "You're fucking kidding me, right?"

I can tell she was expecting a different reaction. She can't hide the flicker of disappointment that runs across her eyes. "No," she says, trying to scare me — and failing. "I'm not kidding. I'm going to kill you."

I roll my eyes so far back that she almost won't need to bother gouging them out if she wants to. I finally leave this fucking cabin, finally go scouting for victims, finally find one, and it turns out that she was also scouting. Just fucking great. I knew it was too easy.

"Un-fucking-believable." I laugh, which I'm sure only confuses her more. "So, this whole time, you were luring me?"

"Yes." She stays still, but her stoic expression is wavering.

"And you picked me out, and came home with me, and intended to kill me this entire time?"

"Yes."

"So, the talking, the flirting, the sex … that was all one big orchestration to kill me?"

"The first two, yes." She's lowered the scalpel by now, but it still rests in her hand and against my hip. "I didn't originally plan the sex, but —"

"You didn't?!" I jerk back up, careful not to jar the scalpel too much. I feel it just barely poke into my hip, and still wince. Christ it's sharp. "You decided to kill me, then changed your mind and decided to fuck me first?" The irony of my anger is not lost on me, but I'm too furious and, frankly, too embarrassed to care.

"Well, why not? It's been a while since I've gotten laid, and well …" She shrugs and smiles a bit. "I wanted to fuck you. You're pretty hot."

See, what did I tell you? It pays to be handsome. Well, except for right now.

Her voice brings me back into focus. "You said you wouldn't kill me now." She presses her hand closer to my hip, and I wince involuntarily, despite the blade not pushing further. "What did you mean by that?"

I'm too focused on the scalpel to answer her right away. It's also too humiliating. I not only have to admit I had almost the exact same reasoning as she did — even down to taking a side trip to have sex first — but I in turn have to admit that I failed at it. She's won, I've lost. And I've lost because of my own stupidity. I deserve to die.

"What did you mean by that?" she asks again, pointing the blade against my side.

I bring my thoughts back to her – well, her scalpel. I'm going to die, but I don't want to sooner than I have to.

"I meant what you probably think," I say, looking her cold in the face. I'm doomed. I'm already tied up. I have nothing left, and nothing to hide. I set my jaw, lift my head up a bit. "I brought you here to kill you."

She doesn't change her expression, and I continue. "Yes, you picked me before I picked you. I picked you after I saw you. I picked you because you were coming onto me, because I wanted you and figured I could get some action before killing you. And yeah, I put it off because I wanted to get laid. I think you're hot too.

"So yes, Candace, I had every intention of murdering you tonight. I mean, Jesus, look around you." I wave my head around the span of the cabin. "Why the fuck do you think I live out here in this godforsaken cabin? It makes it easier to hide people when they're dead!"

"Yeah, I noticed that," she says, interrupting me. "I couldn't believe my luck when you said you lived out in the woods. This place looked like a dream come true when you pulled into the driveway. It's the perfect place to hide you afterward."

See? It's the perfect place to hide the bodies. I'm so good at planning murders, I perfectly planned my own.

"So, I know why you're here, and what you're doing," I continue. "Because it's what I was going to do to you. We're exactly the same."

"Not exactly," she says, coldness entering her voice

once more. She delicately runs the scalpel over my chest. "We were both going to fuck the other one over. But the difference?"

A sudden rush of nausea runs over me, as I guess what's going to happen next: she's going to try and be clever. I swear to God, if she says she came first …

She leans next to my ear. "I came first."

I should've killed her sooner.

"Why?"

She ceases making a long, shallow cut up my chest – the third such cut she's made – and looks up at me, glaring. Her expression matches the cuts she's already made over my skin. Just my luck that I not only pick up a killer, but one who likes to draw out the pain.

"Why what?" she asks, thankfully pausing for a moment. "Why you? Why now?"

"No," I say, breathing deeply and trying to not notice the growing pool of blood on the sheets. She'll have a hell of a time cleaning them up. I hope pieces of me get all over her. Good luck covering your tracks, you cunt. "Why killing?"

She laughs. "My motive? You want me to go all James Bond villain on you?"

"Come on, I'm about to die. If you're not going to kill me straight up, at least talk to me." I shift to bring some feeling back into my ass. One cut has stopped bleeding, but the other three still trickle over my waist. "Why killing? What made you want to do this?"

She looks at me, contemplating whether or not she wants to answer. Despite the circumstances, I can tell that she kind of likes me. It's a liking that I'm sure confuses her. This has been the basis for a lot of my friendships.

"My entire life," she finally says, "involves saving people through very controlled, precise rules."

I raise my eyebrows at her, and she continues, "I really am a nurse. I didn't lie about that. Hell, where do you think I got all this stuff?" She holds up her purse, the source of the rag, the scrubs, the scalpel, and I hope to God nothing else. "It's a profession that found me. All day I'm surrounded by the threat of death, and it's my job to stop it. I always have to stop it. Even when there's no hope."

She sighs, losing her coldness. "It wears on you. I'm supposed to make dying people better. All day I'm covered in blood, in shit and vomit and disease. I have people yell and scream at me, even though I'm trying to help them live. Sometimes in the chaos, I find myself thinking, what if I did the exact opposite of what I'm supposed to do?"

A small smile seeps across her face. "At first, I'd simply imagine mistakes here and there. A slipped scalpel. A fatal medication dose. It's so easy to kill someone in a place that's meant to help people. It's really fascinating, if you think about it. Almost thrilling."

Her eyes are looking away from me now, and I can see her imagining every patient she's treated dying a horrible death. I recognize that look, the one of macabre possibility that only killers possess. I get that look every time I imagine taking someone apart. "You seem like a wonderful nurse," I murmur.

Her attention returns to me. "I actually studied nursing to try to curb that thrill," she explains. "My whole life, I've had fantasies about slipping up, of breaking the rules. What-if scenarios where I'd break something, make it irreversible. Where I'd hurt someone, and they'd never recover." She returns her gaze to me. "Where I'd kill someone, and they'd never come back. I thought maybe if I devoted myself to helping people, I'd stop thinking about ways to hurt them."

Her blade touches my chest, and I feel my pulse quicken. "But I was wrong. It only made it worse. It made me want to do it even more." She looks back at me, holding my eyes with a cold stare. "And it taught me how to do it more effectively."

She makes a quick swipe across my chest. I cry in pain, watching fresh blood spill over. It's always just enough to hurt and bleed, but not to make me pass out or find sweet relief in death. I'm sure she knows that. It's all on purpose.

"So, you've done this a lot," I say, talking through the pain.

"Actually, no," she says, chuckling. "Congratulations — you're my first victim."

Of course, I am. "Great. I feel so special."

"You should." She runs her hand over my cut, tracing blood over my skin. "You're leaving a mark on me, just like I'm leaving them on you. I'll never forget you."

"Awesome. I'm so fucking flattered." I'd love nothing more than to snap off her hand and shove it up her ass right now.

"I just can't believe I bested you in so many ways on my first try. I got to you before you got to me." Her leer turns into a grin. "And I got to make my first kill before you."

Little does she know.

The term "serial killer" implies multiple killings and patterned murders. In this sense, I am not a serial killer. I'd hoped to be, but I didn't meet that criteria.

This is not to say, though, that I am not a killer. That only requires one murder.

My life has always been pretty unremarkable. Well-off parents, reasonably adjusted childhood. I sometimes wonder if my killer instincts subconsciously came from wanting to break up the monotony. All I know is that, at a pretty young age, I stopped seeing people and started seeing their parts.

I still remember the first time this happened. I'd watch my teacher in school and entertain myself by imagining her head floating off her body, her hands suspended in the air still writing on the chalkboard, and her feet tapping silently under the desk. Then one day I imagined taking those pieces apart myself — ripping them off and placing them one-by-one around the classroom. I quickly squelched that fantasy. It was wrong to think that.

I never hurt anyone when I was young. I still listened to adults, people on TV who sent criminals to jail for hurting people. They said that hurting people was wrong. But seeing them in pieces never really went away. It came and went in flickers. I'd do it with strangers, with actors in movies. Kept it at a distance.

I toyed with having those thoughts about my friends. If the thoughts arose, I quickly banished them. Strangers only. No one close. But they kept popping up, and after a while, I let myself have them, if only to make myself feel the horror that came with them. It shocked me to think of my friend's head lying on a carving block. It frightened me to imagine my girlfriend's pussy dissolving over my hand while I fingered her.

I grew concerned when those thoughts stopped being repulsive. I became a little more concerned when I started thinking them intentionally.

Soon, though, they became an escape. Things around me could spin chaotically — my friend could die of cancer, my girlfriend could leave me, people could come and go and school could wear on me and jobs could suck, but I could take it all apart in my mind. It was the only place I could do that, and sometimes, it was the only place I could feel content.

Those fantasies were comforting because they gave me some illusion of control. I could decide if someone lived or died. I could prove to their bodies that I could control their fate. Bodies were too taken with themselves. They could disappear just as easily as they could stand, walk, or talk. I could take them apart, or I could leave them alone. What would it be?

I never fully withdrew, but it did become harder and harder to not imagine the people I spoke to lying in pieces. I shouldn't hurt them. I wouldn't hurt them.

But oh, how I wanted to.

My parents both died suddenly. They were in a car accident. When I heard the news, I didn't even cry. I imagined their car tearing through their bodies. One minute whole, the next in pieces. I only saw their pieces, as they were cremated as soon as I identified them. I never touched them, never took them myself. Something else taken away from me.

One night, a few weeks after they'd died, I went out driving. I drove past the strip malls, the gas stations, the lone Wal-Mart. I wondered how far I could go before I left people behind forever, and how much further I could go before finding them again.

Almost in answer, my eyes chanced upon someone walking ahead on the road. They were walking away from me, strolling casually on the side of the road, as if they did this every day. I only saw them because their white shoes and vinyl jacket shimmered in my headlights. They were alone. Their back was turned to me. They walked as if nothing could hurt them — as if they were in complete control.

I'd show them.

I sped up and jerked the steering wheel to the left. I don't even know if they knew I was coming. They never turned around, not until I'd already hit them. And even then, they didn't turn around so much as land on the hood of my car.

They — or he, as I then saw — ricocheted to the side, and I slammed on the brakes. I turned around, saw him lying on the road.

I ran over him again.

I did it once more for good measure.

I put the car in park. He lay on the road, not moving. I'd killed someone. I'd finally done it.

I looked in my rearview mirror and saw him staying still. He had to be dead. No one would survive being run over three times.

But I had to make sure. I had to control this.

I got out of the car, scooped up his broken body, and placed him in my trunk, his arms crumpling under his torso. As luck would have it, I had some plastic garbage bags back there. It'd make clean-up easier. But where could I take him?

I continued driving forward, figuring these woods would do me well. These woods. They seemed pretty familiar. I drove by a sign with a couple town names. Meadow Rush and Thatcher's Hill. Nature names that probably described some pretty places, but nowhere anyone would actually live. But Meadow Rush rang a bell.

We'll see you next week, son. We're going to the cabin out in Meadow Rush.

The cabin. Mom and Dad had a cabin in the middle of nowhere. I'd gone with them for a month one summer and hated every day of it, but they adored it. It had been their private getaway, a place where they'd go to escape people for a while. Mom would go out there alone and write. Dad would go there and hunt. And as far as I knew, it still stood, unaware that its beloved patrons were reduced to ash and buried closer to civilization.

Fortunately, I now remembered where it was. I turned down a couple of side streets and drove deeper into the woods, until the trees suddenly cleared and there it was.

I got out of the car and looked around. There wasn't a soul for miles. It really was the middle of nowhere. I was amazed there was even electricity. Trees stretched in every direction beyond the clearing, carved only by the road connecting the driveway to the main road. A lone vein to the heart of humanity. Could I sever that too?

I checked to see if the spare keys were in the same place. Sure enough, there they were, under the fake log by the porch. I pocketed them and opened the trunk. My victim was still motionless, still breathless. I picked him up, his arm hanging limply over mine as I carried him to the cabin.

Inside, it was musty and quiet. I flicked on the light and saw everything that had made the place a home away from home for my parents. Furniture, an ancient computer, lamps. The bedroom door was open, and I saw a fully made bed with a linen cabinet next to it. I laid the body on the floor and walked around, finding signs of my parents but no one else. The only sounds around me were crickets, toads, and the occasional bird. There wasn't a soul for miles. I was alone.

Well, not completely alone.

I looked back at the body. It lay in a heap of plastic. He was dead, and I needed to make sure he'd never be found. There were the floorboards. I could just leave him in the cabin, maybe burn this place to the ground or something.

As I thought, my eyes continued scanning the cabin and found the kitchen. They stopped upon a full knife set. I paused, then walked over to it. Despite a light layer of dust, they were in pristine condition.

I returned to the living room with a meat cleaver. He lay on the floor, dead. Was he dead? I was sure he was dead. I had to make sure he was dead.

I could make sure he was dead.

I could control this.

I imagined taking him apart, piece by piece. I imagined burying the parts in precise locations. I could make a pattern, one that spelled out the make of my car or some other clue.

I imagined him broken and buried. And I didn't even try to blink it away. I didn't remind myself that this was wrong. Because here, it wasn't. Here, there was no one for it to be wrong to. There was nobody here — and as such, I could hide anybody in any way that I wanted.

I smiled.

"Why are you smiling?"

I'm staring at the ceiling. I bring myself back to Candace, to the present. I look down and see I'm still bleeding.

"No reason," I say. I won't give her the satisfaction of my own background. "Just remembering things."

I had decided that night that the cabin would be my home, and that killing would be my new normal. It was the only normal I could keep.

But even that hadn't worked out. I never wanted to

leave the cabin, since it was the perfect place to hide. I never saw anything in the news about a missing man. I hid anyway, just in case. I made small trips at night to clear out some essential stuff from my apartment, but otherwise, I abandoned what I had before so I could fully become what I'd always been.

The initial thrill, however, wore off when I realized victims wouldn't just fall in my lap. I had to find them. But I didn't want to. Until I did.

And now I'm here.

I still remember how I felt after that first kill. Years of confusion, suppression, and chaos had been set in order at last. I finally had the control that I craved, that I longed to demonstrate, that I was eager to show others. But I couldn't do that when there was no one around.

And that was the ultimate problem. I couldn't control bodies that weren't there. I had to go to them. And even when I went to them, I couldn't necessarily control what they did to me. Tonight is clear evidence of that.

Maybe tonight is that man's retribution. Maybe I'm learning a cruel lesson about life by losing my own. Maybe it's happening because it's happening and there's absolutely nothing I can do about it. Whatever the reason, I know one thing for sure: I lost.

"Hey!" Candace smacks my leg. Zoning out has become less voluntary. Maybe the blood loss is finally catching up with me. I blink and make eye contact with her, show her I'm still alive — even if not for much longer.

"What?" I manage. "Why do you even want me conscious right now?" Couldn't she just kill me?

"I only want you unconscious," she says, "when I make the right cut."

"So, make it," I say, closing my eyes. "I've got nothing

to say to you."

I feel her grab my hair and lift up my head. I open my eyes, and she's glaring at me. "I'll make it when I'm ready," she says. "I make the rules."

"No, you don't." I gain enough of a second wind to furrow my brow and speak through clenched teeth. "You think you do, but you don't."

"What are you talking about?" She keeps her grip on my hair.

I know I'm talking to myself more than her, but I don't care. "The rules. You think you've made them, or broken them, or made them by breaking them. You haven't. You got me, but because I came to you. You'll kill me, and leave me here, and feel like a success. You can see it all ahead of you, one kill after the other to counter your stupid job. But you don't know what will happen next. You don't know if the cops will find me or find you. You don't know if the person you find next will do the exact same thing to you. You don't know the rules, because in the end, there aren't any. You don't know anything!"

I use my ever-dwindling strength to spit at her. It lands on her face, and she barely flinches. She calmly wipes her face, keeping eye contact with me.

"You're right," she says. Not what I was expecting. It's a running theme this evening. "I don't know what will happen after this. Everyone thinks they know what will happen, that if they do X and Y, that Z will happen. But that's bullshit."

We're so much alike. Maybe in another life, we could've worked together.

"I watch people die every day, people who did X and Y and expected Z, but got something else entirely." She twirls the scalpel against her finger. "They expect me to give them Z. And I have to try my hardest to do so."

She leans towards me. "But not here. Not now. Here and now, I can give whatever answer I want. Here and now, I not only know the answer …" The scalpel leaves her finger, floats to my arm. "… I determine it."

She smiles. "And it feels great."

She makes a sudden slash. I look over and see a long, cascading cut crawling up my entire arm. Blood starts pouring out immediately. As the sight sinks in, she turns and does the same to my other arm. Both cuts long and vertical. Both slashing their respective veins. Both marking the end.

I cry in pain, but that's about the only amount of panic I can muster. I lie helpless, watching my arms drain. Watch her watching me, still smiling. She gets off of me and stands by my side. She runs a palm through my hair, keeps it on my head. Strokes me. "Shh," she says. "It'll be over soon."

I look ahead. I don't want her to see inside me as I die.

I remember the first time I fell asleep in this cabin, during that month from hell with my parents. My heart had raced when the lights went out. I'd never been surrounded by that much darkness. It was suffocating. I'd held my hand in front of me and couldn't even see it. I knew what blindness felt like. I felt trapped under a blanket, one I could claw and tear at, but never rip away.

Now though, I don't panic. I see that blanket as a comfort. The bleeding, Candace's stare, her cuts, the pieces, the loneliness — it'll all be over soon. It'll all be shut out by this darkness; one I now fully embrace.

I close my eyes.

He's gone.

I keep my eyes on him as I grab some rubbing alcohol, pouring it over the scalpel to clean it. He doesn't move; he doesn't breathe. He's no longer here. He's gone — and I took him away.

I smile. All in a night's work.

I leave him tied up. I use his shower. Air-dry instead of using a towel. I've left enough evidence of my presence without adding more. I debate doing a complete scrub-down of the place, but part of me wants to leave clues. More of me also knows no one will ever come looking for him.

I put my bar clothes back on, walking through the various places where I shed them. He was one of the best fucks I've ever had. A shame I'd already decided on his fate. Maybe in another life, we could've lived out here, fucking and killing together. It wouldn't be the worst life. But it wasn't in the cards. Not this time.

My medical supplies are back in my purse. The scrubs I'm not sure what to do with. They're covered in his blood. Laundry will only do so much.

I consider his fireplace, then feel the floor wiggle beneath me as I move towards it. Of course — the floorboards. A classic hiding place, and one without the presence of smoke to draw attention. I'll leave them there. No one will find them. No one else has been here.

I lift up the board and see that I'm mistaken.

Lying underneath of the board is a single, decomposing arm. It still has much of its skin, the fingers gnarled with death. A bit of cloth from a shirt remains. Enclosed by the bit of cloth is an open wound, which is crawling with maggots.

I'm smacked by both the sight and the stench of it and slam the board back into place. I press the board down further with my foot, hoping that's enough to keep the bugs, smell, and as silly as it is, the arm from resurfacing.

He hadn't died victimless — he'd gotten someone. Maybe he got multiple someones.

He could've gotten me.

My heartbeat begins to climb. Part of me thought he was just bullshitting when he said he was going to kill me — that he was just scared or trying to scare me. But his words, the isolated cabin, and most of all the severed arm confirm he wasn't bluffing.

I think about all the times I could've died tonight. The minute we left in his car and drove far away, where no one would see who we were or what we did. As soon as we walked into the cabin, me letting him put his hands wherever he wanted on my body. I remember catching a glimpse at his kitchen while he was going down on me and seeing that collection of knives. I didn't think for one second he'd use them for anything except meal preparation. I didn't think he'd do anything on his bed except sleep and fuck.

I look in the direction of the bed and jump at the sight of him.

Dead. He's still dead. Of course he's dead. I've killed him.

I shudder, thinking he could just as easily have killed me, and keep telling myself that he didn't. I killed him. I dismantled his paint-by-numbers night, injected my own chaos. I won.

Did I?

I can't dwell on it now. I straighten my shoulders, getting myself together. I stuff my scrubs in a plastic bag lying near the kitchen. I'll burn them at home. I do a quick glance through the cabin, looking for any remaining things. I take one final look at him. Still tied up, still covered in blood. Still dead. I hope he'll stay that way.

I grab his car keys from the shelf by the door and make a swift exit. The car will also need to be disposed of, but I'll take care of that later.

I climb in the car and rev the engine, trying not to peel away too quickly. The last thing I want to do is wreck the car before I even get on the highway. I take one final glimpse of the place that almost held me forever, the final resting place of the man who almost got me. The perfect place to leave the body.

I LOVE YOUR WORK

Words meant everything to Ann – especially when they were written by Samuel Miller.

To say that Ann was a bookworm would be an understatement. Even as a little girl, an assortment of authors had passed in and out of her hands – but none had held her quite as tightly as Samuel Miller.

Samuel Miller had floated in and out of Ann's life before she ever read his books. She'd hear his name spoken by her classmates, or see it appear in the credits of a film adaptation of his work. Even though she passed him by on the bookshelves, she could never quite escape him. And even though she'd never read a word he wrote, she had a strange feeling that she should.

When she picked up *First Stop, The Moon*, she felt as if she was visiting a building she'd walked by several times yet never been inside of before. She finished the story, and liked it, although it hadn't held her much while reading it. As time passed, Samuel Miller's story stayed with her. It wouldn't leave her alone.

She felt a small thrill when she was browsing her library and found a copy of *So Says the River*. She'd first heard the title as she'd heard of Samuel Miller, in passing; and when she saw it sitting primly in the library, its blue cover gleaming against the reds and greys of the surrounding hardbacks, she felt as if it was being offered to her. She grabbed it immediately.

So Says the River was a much different experience from *First Stop, the Moon*. Starting with the first page, Ann felt under a spell. Simple words formed elegant sentences, and she found herself immersed in the depths of Samuel Miller's prose. Her heart ached for the story. She felt it in parts of her brain she'd never given to stories before. She'd paused after the final page, staring at the book as if closing it would make it disappear. She'd placed her fingers on the page, touching the final sentences.

She'd vowed, then and there, to read whatever words he wrote. She read more of his books, loving some, feeling indifferent towards others. Even her least favorite stories found their way into her heart. She also followed him on social media and read interviews here and there, combing through the words that hadn't been collected in stories. Samuel Miller's words wrapped themselves around her like a security blanket. He connected with her – but only through the printed page.

In all her years of knowing Samuel Miller, she had never had the chance to meet him. There were opportunities, of course. He often came through her area on book tours, or announced festival appearances, or attended the occasional panel at a convention. But whenever there was a chance to meet him, it seemed like fate intervened to ensure that Ann wouldn't be able to do so. On his last book tour, she had been in New York City the same day he was in town. The local book festival he was to appear at sold out before she had a chance to buy tickets. It seemed to Ann that no matter what, something kept her from meeting Samuel Miller.

So, in her senior year of college, when Ann saw that he was scheduled to do a signing at her local bookstore, she became determined to not let the opportunity pass. She noted the date and quickly scribbled the signing onto her calendar. She already had a copy of the book he was promoting, *A Life in Cinema Cells*, and carefully chose other books of his to bring.

Two days before the signing, Ann was browsing Twitter and saw Samuel Miller post about his appearance: "Friends: don't forget, I'll be at the Olive Branch Bookstore on Thursday, 9 PM to close, signing my new book." Ann smiled, thinking, *I'll be there too.* Her thoughts coursed through her fingertips, and she typed to him in response, "I'll be there. Looking forward to meeting you! I love your work." She'd written him before, and though she knew her words were drowned in the sea of replies he received, she sent them to him all the same, hoping their existence was enough to tell him she was there.

An hour later, as she sat studying for an exam, her phone buzzed. She looked down and, to her delight, saw Samuel Miller's name appear on her phone. He had responded to her tweet: "Thank you Ann. I look forward to meeting you too."

Thank you Ann. His tweet pulsed through her fingertips with the same intensity as his books. He'd seen her words. He'd read them. He'd thanked her for them.

Yes, he was just being polite. No, she wasn't expecting a friendship to blossom between them. His words meant so much to her, though, that she simply wanted him to know that, to know how much his words mattered in her life. He knew and told her so. And tomorrow, she would be able to tell him in person – or so she hoped.

The next morning, Ann was browsing her social networks and saw news from The Olive Branch – there had been a small fire overnight. There wasn't significant damage, but the store would be closed while they assessed the situation.

Ann was crestfallen. A fire? Surely the universe had it out for her. She was glad that no one had been hurt and that the bookstore – one of her favorite places, whether or not Samuel Miller was in it – remained standing. Yet she couldn't help feeling perturbed at what looked to be yet another lost opportunity to meet him.

Ann tried to focus on other things, but her exam notes were gibberish in her current state of mind. She spent the day in a stressed blur and only slept fitfully that night. She checked The Olive Branch's page as soon as she woke up and was delighted to see an update: "We're open! Stop by and say hello. And even better news – Samuel Miller will still be able to attend his scheduled signing. Doors open at 9, so be sure to come by!"

Ann did a small dance on her bed. The store wasn't closed, and Samuel Miller was still coming! Maybe, just maybe, today would be her day. She spent the day's remaining hours in orbit, only coming down from her dream state to study for tomorrow's exam. She sped through dinner, spent some time getting dressed, gathered her books for Samuel Miller to sign, and walked quickly to the bus stop. She'd be there right at nine, maybe a little bit after, but still on time to meet him.

Time passed, but her expected bus didn't arrive. She checked the bus schedule on the stop post, and saw that not one, but two buses should've arrived by now. Where were they?

She pulled up the bus information on her phone and groaned. The bus on this route had been cancelled. Maintenance. *Great*, she thought, *just great. Couldn't they have put up a sign at the damn stop?*

Ann still had time. She pulled up Uber and saw that cars were available. Within five minutes, a driver pulled up and asked if she was Ann.

"Yes, I am," she said as she climbed in. *Nice try, universe.*

She should've known better. They were rolling along

the highway, Ann flipping through *A Life in Cinema Cells*, when she felt the car come to an abrupt stop. "What's going on?" she asked.

"Traffic," the driver answered, not proving to be very helpful.

It's fine, she thought. *Highways have traffic. We'll be moving.*

Time went by, and the traffic didn't ebb. Ann read a whole chapter of her book before she realized they'd barely moved. She arched her neck to look ahead. "What's going on?"

"It looks like there was an accident," the driver said, scrolling through his own phone. "We'll be moving soon, but they're trying to direct everyone around it."

Are you fucking kidding me? Ann looked around her. They were surrounded by cars, trees, and stretches of highway – no exit ramps nearby. *Fuck!*

She slammed her head against the backseat, trying to breathe easier. Worrying wouldn't make the traffic magically go away. She tried reading some more, hoping to take her mind off things; though her heart thumped whenever they moved, and sank when they'd stop a few moments later.

"Are you in a hurry?" the driver asked.

"I'm trying to get to a signing," Ann replied, checking her phone. It was past 9 o'clock. Samuel Miller was already there, probably with a huge line of people. She looked out the window, and wondered if she stared hard enough, the other cars would get going out of fear.

"Well, once I see an exit, I'll get off the highway," the driver offered. "We can get to the bookstore another way."

Ann smiled weakly. He was trying. "Thanks." She picked her book back up, not wanting to talk, and not wanting to focus on her miserable luck.

Slowly but surely, the car began to move more than a few seconds at a time. It was when they picked up speed that Ann dared to look up. They were leaving the highway. The road was clear! Maybe she'd make it after all.

"Okay," the driver said, "I think there's a back way along here, only a couple miles away –"

He'd barely spoken the words when a deer leapt in front of the car. Ann screamed and the driver swerved, barely missing the deer as its hooves glided gracefully over the car. The car was less graceful, swerving and jerking before skidding to a stop. They were okay, but Ann's heart sank as she heard a loud pop under the car.

"Dammit!" the driver yelled as he bolted out of the car. Ann stared blankly ahead of her, wondering what else would keep her away from Samuel Miller.

The driver stood up after a few minutes and tapped her window. She opened the door, and he confirmed what she feared: "It's a flat tire. I don't have a spare either."

Great, just great. She closed her eyes.

"I can cancel the trip, give you a refund ..."

None of those offers would make up for missing Samuel Miller. She sighed and put her head in her hands.

"I'm really sorry."

She looked back up and tried to keep her face calm. It wasn't his fault that everything around her was trying their absolute hardest to keep her from meeting Samuel Miller. "It's okay," she said. "I'm just in a hurry to get somewhere."

"Well, I can't get you there until I call someone to help."

"I know," Ann said, getting out of the car. "Thank you, though, for trying. I'm sorry about your car."

They exchanged goodbyes, and Ann left the driver to

curse over his rotten luck. It was okay, she was only a couple miles away. She could get another car. She pulled out her phone as she walked down the street, ready to make the call, and saw with a sinking heart that her battery was dead.

Okay. No car whatsoever. She looked up the road. She recognized this street. It ended at The Olive Branch. The driver had said they were a couple miles away. When she'd last checked her phone, she'd had a little under an hour before close.

She set her jaw. "I'm coming, Sam."

She strode on the sidewalk as fast as she could. It was dark and growing cool. She saw the moon disappear, and wondered what would happen next. Would a tornado blow through? Would more deer stampede across her path? Would a madman jump out of the woods and kidnap her?

When it happened, it was something less sinister, but no less aggravating. She tripped on a raised piece of sidewalk and skidded across the ground when she landed on it. She turned herself over, examining her scraped palms and scuffed jeans.

"Come on!" she shouted at the trees, having no one else to blame. "What's your fucking problem? Can't you just let me get to the store?" She hung her head, and her eyes welled up. "I just want to meet him. Why is it so hard?"

She looked at her fallen bag. The books hadn't scattered, thankfully, but *So Says the River* peeked out from the top. She blinked back her tears before they could fall and delicately picked up the book. It felt warm in her hands. Comforting. She opened the book to Chapter One and traced her fingers over the words, taking in the power they had over her.

"I will meet him," she said. "I don't care what the universe thinks."

She hoisted herself up, wincing, but not unable to stand. Hoisting her bag over her shoulder, she continued on, barely looking at anything but what was ahead. She ignored the gusts of wind that blew against her, only blinking against a few drops of rain that started to fall. She would not be stopped. The universe seemed to take notice, as the rain remained meek.

At last, she saw a shopping center in front of her, with The Olive Branch gleaming in front. Ann sighed, smiling as she took it in. She trotted to the store, heart thumping. To her relief, the lights were still on, and the door opened. She was here – and so was he. This was actually happening.

She saw a lone sign with an arrow pointing up that proclaimed: "Come upstairs if you want to meet Samuel Miller." *You don't even know the half of it*, she thought with a small smile as she bounded up the stairs. They were closing soon, but they weren't closed, not yet.

She stopped at the top of the stairs, and her eyes widened. There he was. Samuel Miller.

She took him in, and how he towered over both an empty table and the bookstore manager who spoke to him. His dark brown hair rested neatly behind his ears, his deep green eyes shined as he spoke, and his long white fingers placed a brown notebook in a black messenger bag.

Her eyes quickly widened in dismay. Samuel Miller was leaving.

"Wait!"

The word escaped her lips before she'd paused to think how the exclamation, and her disheveled look from the walk and the fall, might make her look crazy. The manager and Samuel Miller both paused, looking up at her in shock.

"I'm here for the signing. I know I'm a bit late, but …"

"I'm sorry," the manager said, "we're closing up shop. The signing's done."

Ann's heart sank, but she continued. She had nothing to

lose. "Please, Jim," she said, stealing a look at his nametag and keeping her tone steady.

She shifted her eyes to Samuel Miller, who looked at her quizzically. "I've wanted to meet you for so long. I love your work."

His eyes fixed steadily on hers. He asked softly, "Are you Ann?"

Her heart soared. He remembered her. "Yes!" she said, beaming. "I'm Ann Monroe, and I love your stories. Just five minutes, please."

"Miss Monroe …" Jim began, but Samuel Miller raised a hand to silence him. "It's all right," he said. "Just one more. I can stay."

Jim paused, nodded, and quietly walked past her. Ann strode to the table where Samuel Miller had taken his seat. The brown notebook was back on the table, alongside two pens.

"Thank you so much," Ann breathed, lifting her books from her bag. "It's such an honor to finally meet you. I've wanted to for so long."

"Not a problem," Samuel Miller replied, smiling at her before turning his gaze to the books she lay in front of him. "I always have time for fans."

He began to sign, and Ann continued as collectedly as she could, "You're my favorite writer. I must've read *So Says the River* –" which Samuel Miller was now signing – "three times at least. It's wonderful."

"Thank you," he said, moving to *A Life in Cinema Cells*. Ann didn't know what to say next but hated the silence. She chuckled softly. "I almost can't believe I'm meeting you. I always seem to miss you. Even tonight, I almost missed you again." He smiled. With a wider grin, she added, "It's almost like something out there was determined to keep me away from you."

"Something probably was," Samuel Miller said softly, finishing his signature.

Ann wasn't sure she'd heard him correctly. Her brow furrowed. "I'm sorry?"

"Something probably was," he repeated, "because it knew what would happen if we met."

She sat in silence. What did he mean by that? He closed the book and looked up at her, smiling; and her confusion vanished. He kept her gaze and asked, "Would you like to see what I'm working on?"

Ann's heart soared. "Yes!" she exclaimed, then flushed at losing her cool. "Yes," she repeated, softer now. He chuckled politely. "Wow, thank you."

Samuel Miller dragged the brown leather notebook closer to them, moving it towards Ann. She held her hand over it. She could almost feel it pulling her to open it. Should she?

"Go ahead," he said. "Take a look."

She hesitated a moment more, then opened it carefully. She saw notes on the pages, an occasional doodle, but mostly scratched-out ideas and stray sentences in need of a home. Even detached from a story, without context and characters, his words were beautiful. She couldn't wait to see the finished product.

"It's in pieces now," he said. "It just needs one more bit, and then it'll be ready."

"Like what?" she asked absently, turning the pages. She could even get lost in his notes. Outside she heard a sudden gust of wind. It almost sounded like a sigh.

"Like you."

This got her attention. She looked up at him.

His face stayed neutral, but his eyes blazed. Ann felt uneasy, yet unable to move or let go of the page.

"I need you, Ann."

Her body grew cold. "I don't understand," she said.

"You always hear writers say they couldn't do what they do without their fans." He calmly lifted his other pen. "They mean it, in their own way, but it's still just a figure of speech." His eyes locked onto hers. "Not for me."

He clasped her wrist, and she barely jumped, so intense was his stare. "I couldn't do what I do without my fans," he continued, "because then what I do wouldn't exist. I need them, Ann. I need you." He smiled warmly, dangerously; her heart began to race. "And at last, I have you."

Her trance was broken by a searing pain across her palm. She looked down and saw his pen hovering above her hand. It took a second longer to realize he wasn't holding a pen, but a knife. Her hand was bleeding onto the page.

Her mouth dropped open, but she only managed to breathe quickly. Screaming was seemingly out of her reach. Samuel Miller's grip was strong, and she watched as her blood dripped on his words. He turned her arm and pressed her palm onto the notebook. The page seared her quickly, a burn that faded into a stronger version of the sensation she felt when she'd read his books, when she'd touched his words.

Next to her hand, the notes and scribbles began to move. They swam in her blood, swirling and twisting as they changed from notes into sentences, scribbles into prose. They surfaced anew as the words which sustained her for years. As they completed themselves, she looked back at her hand and saw it was gone. She was wrist-deep in the notebook, and felt herself being pulled further and further in. Pages flipped and the sensation intensified as each paragraph completed itself. Everything around her was fading quickly. She finally managed a scream. At last, the notebook snapped shut, and Samuel Miller held it in his hands.

"Thank you, Ann." He packed his pens and notebook and stood up to depart.

Jim came back upstairs, his voice entering a few moments before him. "Okay Miss Monroe, Mr. Miller," he called. "It's past close, we really have to –"

Jim stopped, looking at the empty table. Samuel Miller finished buttoning his coat, looking at Jim casually. Jim stood, looking confused. "Where'd she go?" he asked. "I didn't see her leave."

"Who?" Samuel Miller replied, looking at Jim calmly. "I was just packing up."

Jim stood still, wondering. His brow lost its furrow. "Oh," he said at last. "Right. The last guy left a while ago. That's right."

Samuel Miller smiled. Of course that was right. He was the author. He controlled the story.

"Well, thank you for coming, Mr. Miller," Jim continued. "Your driver's out front."

"Thank you," Samuel Miller replied. He swept past Jim and exited the store. He entered the waiting car and pulled out his notebook as he rode to his hotel, writing one final piece: *Ann went missing, but nobody looked for her.*

THE CROW'S GIFT

Tabitha loved the variety of birds she saw every morning on her walk to school. Now in 4th grade, she walked alone; however, as a small child, her mother had walked with her and taught her how to name each bird she saw along the way: sparrows, blue jays, wrens and robins. They hid in trees and danced on the gravel. They picked up worms from rain-soaked sidewalks and shared the branches with foraging squirrels. Her walk to school would've been lonely now if it weren't for the birds. She loved their company, and she loved them all — even the crows.

The crows were different from the others. She'd see them in groups, but only with each other. They stayed atop telephone phones or tucked into trees with no other birds or creatures. Perhaps they liked to be left alone. Or maybe they wanted friends, and the other animals kept them away.

Tabitha knew how that felt. Her classmate Jane sometimes had space for her at the lunch table. And many children quietly agreed if she asked to play. But no one asked her to play with them. No one sat at her table at lunch. No one invited her to their house after school.

No one actually wanted to be her friend.

Tabitha thus felt sorry for the lonely crows and tried her best to be their friend. When she walked past them, she'd wave and say, "Hello!" She suspected the crows didn't speak English, but it was her hope that they knew, in their own way, that she was greeting them. That she was acknowledging them, and saw them as friends.

Her efforts were rewarded one morning when a silent crow suddenly squawked as she walked by.

Tabitha felt a rush of excitement but brushed it off. It was a bird — birds made noise. She still greeted him. "Hello!" she said, waving.

Two squawks this time, and a flap of his wings.

It couldn't be. Could it?

Tabitha smiled all the rest of the way to school. Even if it was just pretend, it was nice to think that she had made a new friend.

"Hey look, it's Terrible Tabitha."

Simon's taunts were mean, but not very creative. Creativity required intelligence. As usual, Tabitha kept her eyes averted in an attempt to ignore him, and his horrible friends who snickered at his every word.

Most of the children left Tabitha alone. But not Simon. Tabitha didn't know when or why Simon had chosen to be mean to her. Most days she could ignore him, but that didn't stop the gnawing sadness that grew when she saw him at school. His torment had grown out of nowhere. Now it was so ingrained in their routine that she simply saw it as something true, like the sun rising each morning or the birds migrating each winter.

Simon always started the day by finding something about her to mock — usually her secondhand clothes, or her large glasses, or her flat pale hair, or the small amount of pudge around her middle. He cycled through them in such a pattern that she wondered if he had a collection of socks with different "Insults for Tabitha" stitched on them for each day.

Today it was clothing. "Where did those pants come from? Goodwill's reject pile?" More laughter. Tabitha kept her back to them, wishing she could stop the slow flush rising up her cheeks. She was saved by the arrival of their teacher, Miss Patterson. Simon was cruel and stupid, but not enough of either to bully Tabitha in front of a teacher.

The school day passed as normal, including more mockery from Simon at lunch. Rather than listen to his taunts, she'd sequestered herself in the library, leaving her lunch unfinished and her mind preoccupied with shame and loneliness. Her distraction remained during her lessons, making the hours pass all the more slowly. The final bell rang like music in her ears, and she walked home, shuddering against the growing chill in the wind.

She gathered rocks as she walked, the stones ranging from mundane to beautiful. She liked decorating her windowsill with them. As she pocketed her gathered stones, she noticed one of the crows standing on a fence post.

"Hello!" she said, waving her fingers.

Squawk! A flap of his wings. Surely that was an answer — it wasn't possible that could happen twice. She smiled. Maybe she did have a new friend.

Tabitha remembered some uneaten crackers in her lunchbox. "Are you hungry?" she asked. The crow didn't squawk or flap, but stood still, watching her. She reached into her lunchbox and pulled out a cracker. Still seeing no response from the crow, she placed it on the ground slowly.

Squawk! As she backed away, the crow swooped down onto the cracker, grabbing it and returning to his post in a single loop. He swallowed the cracker, flapped his wings, and squawked again. Then he flew away.

Tabitha smiled. Even though it was brief, and with a bird, it was nice to have a friendly interaction that day. She left three whole crackers in a line on the post, in case the crow or his group returned. In her mind, she named him Timothy.

Tabitha and her mother lived in an unremarkable home; a single story surrounded by a barren lawn. It's what they could afford. Tabitha never knew her father. She used to ask her mother about him, but she only received clipped answers and teary eyes. She couldn't help but wonder if those conversations were one of the reasons her mother stopped walking with her to school. She learned to make it a point not to upset her, if that's what it took to keep her close.

Despite her best efforts, though, Tabitha often saw how sad her mother was. Today was no exception. Tabitha saw her mother cooking, occasionally wiping her eyes between stirring the pot. She watched her mother silently, not wanting to disturb her. She knew it embarrassed her mother when Tabitha saw her cry, and Tabitha didn't want to sadden her further. After watching her for a few moments, she turned back around the corner, leaning against the wall and listening for signs that dinner would be ready soon.

"Tabitha!" her mother called. She heard the skillet start to sizzle, bowls clinking onto the counter. "Come set the table, please."

She scurried into the kitchen, and her mother, red-eyed but otherwise appearing all right, laughed with a start. "Right there!" she exclaimed. "Were you outside the kitchen the whole time?"

"I'd just come near the door," Tabitha lied.

Her mother smiled. "My little ghost." Tabitha grinned. She looked at the counter and saw dinner. Grilled cheese and soup – one of her favorites. Her mother saw it as basic food, poor food, but Tabitha loved it.

"Put the bowls and plates on the table, please," her mother said. "The sandwiches are almost done."

Tabitha did as she was told, placing everything perfectly. She didn't want to spill soup or leave any spoons askew on the napkin. A nice table usually made her mother smile.

No sooner had she sat in her chair than her mother turned off the oven and carried a hot skillet of fresh sandwiches to the table. Tabitha watched hungrily as the sandwiches slid onto their plates. She immediately tucked into her sandwich, not bothering to wait for it to cool.

"How was school today, darling?" her mother asked, slowly sipping her soup.

"It was fine." She talked a bit about some of her lessons. Tabitha usually left her school stories short. She didn't want to trouble her mother with stories about Simon. Her mother listened quietly, sipping soup and giving an occasional "Mm hmm." Tabitha knew her mind was elsewhere, on whatever had been making her cry before.

She wondered if hearing about the crows would cheer her mother up. "I also made a new animal friend after school today."

Her mother looked up. "A new animal friend?"

"Yes," Tabitha said, "a crow. A big black one, with shiny wings. I've named him Timothy."

"Timothy," her mother replied. "A strong name."

"Yes." Tabitha was glad to see her mother was interested. "I said hello, and he squawked at me. He even flapped his wings, like he was waving at me."

"Crows are very intelligent birds. I bet he recognized you."

"That's what I thought! And I saw him after school and gave him a cracker. He squawked again and ate it and then flew away, so I left three more for him and his friends."

"Be careful feeding them, Tabitha." Her mother's face grew serious. "That was very nice, but he could've bitten or scratched you."

Tabitha's face flushed. She'd been trying to cheer her mother up and instead made her worry. "I was careful," she said, her eyes cast down on her plate. "I put the crackers on the ground first."

"Oh. That's good, then. You're a smart little girl."

Tabitha smiled. All was well.

"You mentioned Timothy and his friends," her mother said, sipping her water. "Do you know what a group of crows is called?"

"Just a group, right?" Tabitha asked.

"No. Something more sinister." Her mother smiled slyly. "They're called a murder of crows."

"A murder!" Tabitha's eyes widened in shock, yet she couldn't help but grin with glee. A murder sounded so forbidden.

"That's right." Her mother dabbed her mouth with a napkin, her soup gone and her sandwich mostly finished. "Crows are quite friendly, as you saw today. But make sure you're friendly to them. They remember kindness, but they also don't forget cruelty – just like people."

Tabitha nodded. "I would never hurt them," she declared. "Timothy's my friend. I'd never hurt him or his friends."

Her mother patted her hand. "And I'm sure they'll never hurt you. Kindness speaks volumes." She turned from Tabitha and looked out the window, seeing everything but what was outside. Tabitha's shoulders fell. Despite her best efforts, she'd lost her mother yet again.

"I'll clear the table," Tabitha said, wishing that people had been kinder to her mother.

The next morning, Tabitha walked to school with the most happiness she'd felt since she started walking alone. She hoped to see Timothy and the rest of his murder. Hopefully the growing cold hadn't scared him away. Did crows fly away for the winter?

If so, then they hadn't left yet. When Tabitha rounded the corner, walking near the old fence post, she heard a loud squawk. She looked at the tree it had come from, delight crossing her face.

"Good morning, Timothy," Tabitha called, waving.

Squawk! He flapped his wings this time. Tabitha thought for sure he was waving. He flew across her, landed on the fence post, and let out another loud squawk, pointing his beak at the post. Was he beckoning her?

Tabitha walked to the post, and Timothy took flight, but only to a nearby branch. She gasped when she looked at the post. Lying upon it were three colorful stones, neatly polished. They looked like the stones she collected, but nicer, less blemished.

She bet he'd found them far off in the woods, somewhere only an animal would think to look.

"They're beautiful!" she exclaimed. She quickly pocketed them and looked at Timothy in gratitude. He cocked his head at her. "Thank you!" she cried, waving.

Squawk! He took flight, soaring into the thickest trees. Tabitha stuffed her hands into her pockets, keeping the stones pressed against her fingers. She vowed to pocket more of her crackers during lunch.

"All right class." The lights went out, and voices hushed. "Please direct your attention to the board."

Tabitha normally did this, but not today. She was too distracted. A crow had brought her a gift. In just 24 hours, a bird had shown her more kindness than her classmates had shown her all year.

"Today," Miss Patterson continued, "we'll be learning about birds."

This brought Tabitha's attention back to the board. On the wall, she saw a projection of an assortment of birds. Miss Patterson clicked through, and an albatross came up. "Who can tell me what this bird is?"

"Albatross," the class recited, and Tabitha continued to only listen with half an ear. She guessed Miss Patterson would go through the birds alphabetically. Sure enough, a short time later she heard the class answer, "Bluebird." She doodled in her notebook.

However, upon hearing "Crow," she looked straight up. A painted picture of a crow stood in front of her. It looked small compared to Timothy.

"Yes, a crow," Miss Patterson said. "Not to be confused with a raven — crows are much smaller." Tabitha didn't think Timothy was as big as a raven, but he did have a good size to his feathers. Maybe the crow on the board was a girl.

"Can anyone tell me what they know about crows?" Miss Patterson asked.

Multiple hands shot up, including Tabitha's. Tabitha normally preferred to hide her answers from Miss Patterson's attention and Simon's taunts; but seeing the crow – an image of her friend – made her feel brave.

Miss Patterson, however, saw her other classmates first. She pointed at various students, who answered with the basics. "They're black!" said Susan. "They eat dead things!" said Jason. "They travel in groups!" said Jane.

"They're not called groups!" Tabitha shouted. She knew she'd spoken out of turn, but she was too excited to care. Miss Patterson turned in her direction, her eyes wide. "A group of crows is called a murder."

"Very good, Tabitha," Miss Patterson said, her look of shock becoming pleasant surprise. "She's right. A flock of crows is called a murder."

Tabitha beamed, proud to be praised in front of her classmates. "They're also very intelligent," she continued, unable to stop herself. "They recognize people. They know when you're nice and when you're mean, and they remember."

"That's stupid," said Simon, his voice cruel and familiar in the dark. Tabitha's joy clattered to the floor, breaking into pieces. "Animals are too dumb to know that stuff."

"Actually, Simon — Tabitha's right," Miss Patterson said. "Crows are highly intelligent creatures. They remember a lot more than other birds — and even some people."

"Like you, Simon," said Jason. A portion of the class laughed, and Miss Patterson scolded them. Simon's silence spoke more harshly to Tabitha than anything he could say. She knew he'd been embarrassed, and even though Jason insulted him, she'd be the one to pay for it.

"Okay, moving on from crows," Miss Patterson continued once the class had settled down, "who can tell me what this bird is?"

As the rest of the class said, "Dodo," Tabitha returned to silence and her doodles. She sketched a picture of Timothy to take her mind off Simon and her classmates. Soon school would be over, and she could see her real friend.

Tabitha clutched the crackers she'd saved from lunch in her pocket. She'd deliberately saved them this time, though it had been difficult. She figured an emptier stomach was worth it if it meant being kind to a friend.

As she rounded the corner, she saw four crows aligned on the fence post. Upon seeing her, three flew up to the tree. One stayed behind. *Squawk!*

"Hello, Timothy," Tabitha replied. She walked up to the fence. Timothy inched back but stayed on the fence. She was tempted to feed him a cracker from her hand, but she remembered what her mother had said about bites and scratches. Timothy could do either, even by accident. She instead placed the cracker on the fence. Timothy skittered to it quickly, once again downing the cracker in one gulp. *Squawk!*

"You like them, do you?" Tabitha asked, smiling.

"Are you talking to a bird?"

Tabitha jumped at the familiar sound of Simon's cruel voice, a sound she'd thought she'd escaped upon leaving school.

"What are you doing here?" she asked. He didn't live anywhere nearby.

"Is that your crow friend?" he continued, ignoring her. "Hoping he remembers all the nice things you do?"

"I …" She was always at a loss for words around Simon. "I like to feed him, is all. He's kind to me."

Simon sneered. "It would take a dumb animal to be nice to you. Birds of a feather, right?" He laughed at his stupid joke. Tabitha remained quiet, looking at her feet.

Timothy, on the other hand, spoke up. *Squawk, squawk!* He had moved to a post further away but stayed close enough to flap his wings in Simon's direction, voicing his discontent.

Simon quickly scooped a rock from the ground. "Get out of here, you stupid bird!" Before Tabitha knew it, the rock was airborne, sailing in a straight line towards Timothy.

Fortunately, Timothy was fast — he cleared the post, allowing the rock to sail under his feet. Simon bent down to gather more rocks while Timothy retreated towards the tree.

"No!" Tabitha cried. "You'll hurt him!" She grabbed Simon's arm to try and stop him.

Timothy disappeared into the trees, and Simon wrested his arm from Tabitha's clutch, sending her to the ground. Her glasses fell from her face. She felt her hands scrape as she landed on the rough dirt. Before she could reach them, Simon strode to her glasses and stomped them twice, shattering the lenses.

"See if your crow friend is smart enough to fix this for you," he said, and laughed as he ran off.

Tabitha stayed on the ground until he was out of sight, then sat up and leaned against the fence post. Her palms were bleeding. She picked up the remains of her glasses. Replacing them would be another expense, another burden. She dug a small hole and buried their remains, devising a quick lie to tell her mother about their whereabouts. She'd simply say she lost them. Her mother didn't need to know that someone broke them, someone whose cruelty seemingly followed her wherever she went – even to places where she had found kindness.

She cried quietly. She cried for her glasses, for her mother, for her own pride. Kindness shouldn't be so hard to come by, nor cruelty so easy.

Squawk!

Tabitha looked to her left. Timothy stood on the ground a few feet away. He looked at her quizzically. She wiped her tears. Even if the world wasn't kind, Timothy was — and she could be too. She unearthed the remaining crackers from her pocket — several crushed into pieces — and spread them out over the lower fence post.

"For you and your friends," she said.

Timothy looked at the crackers, then flew to a higher post. He descended again, then dropped a smooth grey stone on the ground. He then flew away.

Tabitha forced a smile and pocketed the stone. She rose to her feet and started to walk home, preparing to face her mother. She looked behind her and saw Timothy and four other crows dining on the crackers. Timothy looked up, caught her eye, and flapped his wings.

Tabitha had walked to school in silence the next morning, her heart and eyes in pain. She was back to wearing an old pair of glasses from a year or two ago until she could get new ones. They were too tight and gave her a headache, but it was what she had to deal with.

She hadn't seen Timothy or the other crows. It was just as well — she didn't feel like talking to anyone or anything that day. So it was just her luck that today of all days, Jane rushed to talk to Tabitha as soon as she spotted her in the halls.

"Tabitha!" she yelled. Tabitha tried to ignore her and pretend she hadn't heard, but Jane quickly followed her. "Tabitha, did you hear the news?"

"What news?" Tabitha asked glumly, resigning herself to having to be social.

"About Simon!"

This got Tabitha's attention. She stopped and turned to face Jane, who was wide-eyed and obviously eager to share the news. "No," she said, hoping it was that he'd moved away. "What about him?"

"He was attacked last night," Jane explained, "by wild birds."

Tabitha's own eyes widened. "Wild birds?"

"Yeah!" Jane couldn't hide the hint of excitement behind her tale of horror. "He was throwing rocks at birds last night, and these crows suddenly swooped on him. It was one big one, and then another, until they were all over him."

Tabitha couldn't speak. Jane continued as they walked towards their class. "They were scratching and pecking and everything, and he couldn't get up. They finally left when his mother and brother came outside — they told my mother, that's how I heard, because his brother had to stay with us while his parents took him to the hospital."

"The hospital?" Tabitha asked, and they stopped just outside of their classroom door. "For pecks and scratches?"

"It wasn't just pecks and scratches." Jane looked around her, then dropped her voice to a whisper. "They gouged one of his eyes out."

Tabitha said nothing. Jane took her silence for disbelief, and said, "It's true, I heard his mother say so. She said he'll have a patch for the rest of his life."

The bell rang, and Jane slipped into the classroom. Tabitha stood still a few moments longer. It had to be a crazy rumor. Jane must've misheard Simon's mother.

She walked into the classroom and noted Simon's empty desk. She sat quietly, thinking about Jane's story. Maybe it could be true after all.

Tabitha stayed away from home after school ended. She leaned against the fence post, deep in thought, watching as the sky turned pink and orange with streaks of blue. She would be home before dark, but she wanted to stay out a little longer.

She stared into the trees and the bramble. There were fewer birds every day, and the evenings grew quieter as winter strolled in. Tabitha felt the wind stinging her cheeks. Soon she wouldn't be able to stay outside for long. Neither would the birds.

She wondered if Timothy and his friends had already left. Perhaps they moved south to get warm. Perhaps they'd fled after what happened to Simon. Surely Simon's mother had called animal control — though Tabitha didn't know how effective they'd be against birds. She hoped animal control hadn't found them or wouldn't bother trying.

Squawk!

Tabitha did not jump or start. Deep down, she'd known they hadn't left. She'd known they'd come to see her. Deep down, she'd known Jane's story was true.

She turned her head to her left, and saw Timothy alight onto the fence post. She looked at him in silence. She continued watching as Timothy laid what was in his beak on the post.

She knew she should feel sorry for Simon, and chase Timothy and his friends away. Tabitha knew how everyone else would feel had they been there. She knew how Miss Patterson would react, or Jane, or even her mother.

She, however, could not react the way they would. She couldn't ignore the crows nor reject them. She knew that in their own way, the crows had been kind to her. It was their nature – as well as hers.

She gave a small smile. "Thank you, Timothy."

Squawk! Timothy cocked his head, and Tabitha swore it was in salute. After a moment, Timothy quietly fluttered away.

Tabitha watched the trees, listening for any squawks or rustling of wings. Perhaps she'd see them tomorrow. She'd wave to them if they appeared. She'd continue to bring them crackers and appreciate the gifts they brought her.

She slowly looked away, grateful for their friendship, and closed her hand over a single eye.

WITHER

Katie sang to herself as she walked through the woods, looking for something to eat. She'd walked this path as long as her family lived in their cottage, the woods offering an abundance of berries, vines, and roughage to line their stew pot. Katie's stomach growled as she remembered her father's pheasant stew, made all the more delicious by crushed juniper berries and dandelion stems steeped in the broth. "Gives it something extra," he'd say with a wink as he sprinkled black pepper into the mix. Something extra to make her mouth water. Something special to share with her family.

Now she had nothing to share, and no one to share it with. Katie looked back at the cottage, a small dot at the end of a stretch of grass, like an errant pimple on a stretch of skin. Her parents hadn't walked with her in months, even before the hunger and illness that Katie felt within her had taken her parents away. They lay within the cottage, still and dead upon their mattress. She could still hear their voices, still hear them tell her how the city they'd left was worse than the woods. She could still hear her mother sing lullabies to her to help her sleep when she was little. Katie sang those lullabies now, sang them in a whisper to give herself a sense of comfort as she tried to live a little longer.

Katie had lived in the woods almost all of her life, but not long enough to completely forget the life she'd had before. The one in the wicked place, clogged with smoke and noise and the chatter of people. Katie remembered them in flashes, almost like dreams she'd dreamt as a child and carried with her in her teenage years. She mostly remembered them as nightmares, a nightmare her parents shared with her in their cramped townhouse. Her mother's textbooks loomed like towers as she prepared tests for her students, and her father's hands held dirt and the scent of brown paper grocery bags when he came home from his shift at the co-op. She even remembered her grandmother's hands, as little as she'd seen them. They often stroked her hair or gave her colorful candy, gummy bears that Nana said were good for her. "They have vitamins," she told her.

"What are vitamins?" Katie asked.

"Something good for you."

Katie took them, trusting that her grandmother, like her mother, would only give her things that were good for her.

Her mother didn't like the vitamins. She spoke of them the way she and her father spoke of the city they lived in: lacking. Unhealthy. Wicked. "You don't need those," her mother told her when Katie had asked if they could buy some.

"Nana says I do," Katie said with a fixed stare – her first act of defiance, something she didn't realize at five years of age. Her mother stared back at her with coldness, and Katie realized that she said something wrong. Her mother didn't speak a word, but Katie still felt a chill that settled on her heart and told her through its pulsing that to defy one's mother was to defy one's blood.

Thus, Katie said nothing more. She said nothing in the weeks ahead as her mother and father packed things in boxes and took them away. She listened in silence as they ate dinner and her parents talked about the lack of health in the wicked place, and how they didn't want any part of it. She looked out the car window without a word as they packed their final boxes and drove away from the city. Katie didn't realize until they'd reached the woods that she would never see the city or the people within it again.

The city, and their home within it, wilted in Katie's memory. She replaced those images with their cottage in the woods, replaced the scents of the city with flowers, bark, and fresh meat her father brought to their kitchen. They ate every day. They managed to stay warm in winter and gardened in spring and summer. Katie grew used to the woods and remembered that first year even in the second year, when she first went to bed with a growling stomach.

Katie couldn't ignore the growls, even when she told herself that what they had was enough. Her mother and father insisted that what they had was enough. Katie didn't dare say otherwise. She remembered too clearly the look on her mother's face when she'd asked for more of what Nana had given her. She didn't want to feel its effects again.

However, she didn't want to feel the painful hollow in her stomach. "Mom?" she called.

Her mother came right away.

"I can't sleep," Katie said.

Her mother sat on the bed with her. "Is something wrong?"

"Can you sing to me?" Katie liked to hear her mother

sing.

"Won't singing keep you awake?"

"It'll help me go to sleep. Please?"

Her mother laughed a little, then began to sing. Katie's stomach interrupted her song. Katie worried the growl would upset her, but instead, her mother laughed again. "Are you a little hungry?" she asked.

Katie nodded. "Do we have anything extra to eat?"

"Not until morning. Not if we want enough to last through the winter."

Katie remembered winter in the city. There was much more food, boxes of cereal and macaroni and cheese bursting from their cupboards. Her mouth began to water at the memory.

"No matter what we have to eat," her mother said, "or what we don't have, we'll always have something, because we have each other."

"Will we have the city again?" Katie asked, pulling her blanket up to her chin.

Her mother chuckled. "You can't have a city. You can live there."

"I liked living there. We had more food."

"The city is a wicked place. And more isn't always better. Do you remember the plants I showed you during our lessons today?"

"The ones with three leaves? The ones I can't touch?"

"That's right. They're poison, and they spread their poison along your hands and fingers." Her mother tickled her, and Katie shrieked with glee despite her mother's tale of horror. "They spread when fingers touch the oils, and creep along your skin. The ivy crawls along the earth, growing even though it isn't wanted. Cities do what poison ivy does, and poisons more than just our skin. They poison the earth."

"With a rash?"

"You could say that. People can be just as pesky as poison ivy." Her mother looked out the window, her lips pursing as she thought of all the people she and her father wanted to keep Katie away from. "The earth provides us so much, and we respond by poisoning the thing that gives us life."

"And gives us rashes."

Katie's mother looked at her. "What?"

"The earth makes poison ivy, right? It poisons us."

"No Katie, she keeps us alive."

"So, she does both?"

"No." She chuckled, and Katie detected frost on her laughter's tail end. "The earth makes things which are poisonous. But if we know what to avoid, and how to care for what sustains us, then we'll be sustained."

Katie furrowed her brow, her mother's words ringing hollow in her six-year-old ears. Her mother clarified, "If we pick the right things, then the earth will do right by us."

Katie smiled. "Okay."

"And the earth will do right by us if we do right by her." Her mother smiled back, and a deeper passion flickered in her eyes. Katie flinched under its strength. "And she'll do wrong to the people who don't."

Their years in the woods stretched on. They almost never went to the city, and even then, only Katie's father would go. Katie sometimes went with him when she was little and could fit in a bike seat. She loved the breeze as he sped along the trail connecting their cabin to the city. "We're just getting a few things the woods can't provide," her father always said when they stopped at the recycling center for old newspapers, a used bookstore for books on foraging, or the co-op for spices.

As Katie grew, it grew more difficult for her to go with him. She was too big for the seat, and too big for her father to carry both her and their wares back home. Her father told her many times she couldn't go, but one day, she felt an unexpected sadness when her father told her to stay in the woods. "But I want to go!" she protested.

"You're too big for the bike seat," her father repeated.

"Then let me ride into the city. I can ride a bike. I know what you need."

"Nine's too young to ride to the wicked place alone," her father clucked, though Katie detected tension in his voice.

"But –"

"Katie." Her mother's voice broke through them like wind through a field. She walked towards them and put her hand on Katie's shoulder. Katie could almost feel her mother's power creep across her back and spread over her skin. Her mother's control didn't scare her, though. It felt comforting, a feeling of nurture she felt when her mother sang her lullabies or gave her an extra piece of bread at dinner.

"Your father can go to the wicked place," she said. "I need you to help me forage."

Katie nodded. She and her mother gathered their baskets while her father left to get more newspapers. He brought less food from the city with each trip, for both he and her mother found more value in what they found in the woods.

Katie had trouble seeing that value when all she saw were leaves and dirt. "I'm tired of bark," she said with a pout as they walked down the path. "It's all we can find in the woods."

"Not necessarily," her mother said. She crouched to the

ground and pushed back the branches of a bush. Katie gasped when she saw dots of red clustered in the grass.

"Wild strawberries!" Katie exclaimed.

"That's right. I knew you'd remember from your lessons." Her mother began to pick the fruit. "The woods will provide. We simply have to look for its provisions."

"What's a provision?" Katie asked as she rummaged through leaves on the ground, making sure to avoid any with three leaves.

"Something you need." She dropped the wild strawberries into Katie's basket. "Like this fruit, which will give you vitamins and make you strong. These are much better than anything from the wicked place, because the earth made them."

"Like the greens we had last night?"

Her mother smiled as she dropped more strawberries in the basket. "Yes, sweetheart. Exactly."

"Or these mushrooms?" Katie reached for a patch of yellow toadstools shining by a log.

"Katie, don't!"

Katie stopped even before her mother's hand grabbed hers. Katie looked at her. Her mother's hold softened, but her eyes remained frantic.

"Not those," she said, releasing Katie's fingers. "They're poisonous."

Katie frowned. "But they're mushrooms. We eat them."

"We don't eat those mushrooms."

"How am I supposed to know what kind we can eat? They all look the same!"

"Actually, they don't. The earth is very good to us. She tells us which mushrooms we should and shouldn't eat based on a variety of things. Shape, color, the list goes on."

Katie sighed. She was young enough to respect

everything her parents said, but old enough to still grow frustrated by them. "And does the earth tell us what shapes and colors are bad?"

"Yes. And so do books – which is why your father brings them back for us. Let's go over mushrooms tomorrow for your lessons."

Katie was a fast learner, which served her well for her daily lessons with her mother. Learning quickly meant going back outside and finding what more the woods could provide, or setting aside her mother's dusty textbooks in favor of the newspapers her father brought home. Katie loved to read the papers from beginning to end, even when the news was sad, like when wars began in far-off cities, or when someone from their own city died of a mysterious illness officials had traced to her food.

Katie didn't want to be poisoned by food and thus paid rapt attention to her mother's lessons on foraging. The expansion of Katie's wilderness studies was going well. She no longer reached for poisonous mushrooms or deceptive berries.

Katie also liked to see her mother's happiness as they pored over the science books. Biology was her mother's favorite subject, and she stroked the pictures of plants in the book as if they were growing in the dirt outside. Her mother pointed at a drawing of a lily. "That's my favorite flower," she said, her finger resting on its petals. "I haven't seen one in years."

"They don't grow here?" Katie asked.

"No."

Katie touched the painted stem. She remembered

touching one before, long ago. "I think I remember seeing them all the time when I was little."

"That's because we had them in our garden."

"Our garden!" Katie's eyes shined at the memory. It had been filled with all sorts of natural delights, from lilies to tomatoes. "Why don't we have one here?"

"Because the forest is our garden." Her mother turned the page, keeping her eyes on the book.

"But couldn't we grow things outside of the cottage? Like lilies or kale or even marigolds?"

"No. In the city, we needed a garden to keep nature alive. Here, the earth does it for us."

Katie remembered the barren paths of winter that she and her parents had foraged without success for the past few years. She rolled her eyes. "When it feels like it, anyway."

Her mother snapped the book shut. Katie felt a chilled wind burst from its pages.

"It feels like it," her mother said, her voice a hiss that slithered across the table and wrapped around Katie's heart. "*She* feels like it, when she feels cared for. It's not up to you. Her gifts are yours to respect, not yours to command. Understand?"

"Yes." Katie was too hungry to argue. She wondered if her father's stew, a bare concoction of simmered bark and dried mushrooms, would be ready soon.

"Let me show you something." Her mother pulled another book between them, a biology textbook with yellowed pages and the year 1974 blotted but visible in the bottom corner. Katie wondered for a moment why her mother needed a textbook more than forty years old for their lessons.

Her mother opened the book and showed her a drawing of a beetle on a plant. "These beetles are pests," her mother explained. "They destroy these plants, and at greater numbers than necessary for the natural balance."

"Do other animals eat them?"

"Yes. Sometimes though, it isn't enough – especially when their predators are hunted or shoved out by people cutting down the forest for their homes."

"So, what happens when the beetles aren't eaten?"

"The plants take matters into their own hands."

"How?"

"They restructure themselves so that they become poisonous to the beetles."

"They become poisonous?"

"Yes. To the beetles. They sense they're being destroyed, and not in tune with the balance of the earth. So, they attack their attackers." She scooted the book towards Katie, who frowned at its pages. "Neat, huh?"

"I guess – though that sounds a little out there."

"It's not. They're evolving to survive and punishing those who interfere with the earth's ability to provide. It's resilience in its finest form." Her mother stroked her hair, and Katie felt tingles rain down her skin like shards of glass. "It's what makes nature so beautiful."

"Daphne, Katie," her father called. "Dinner's ready."

Her mother removed the books, making way for bowls of their winter stew. Katie kept the science book tucked under her chair and took it with her to bed later that night. She opened the book to read more about plants, to see if what her mother said was actually possible. Her research on poisonous plants stopped, though, when she chanced upon drawings of a naked boy and girl.

Katie grabbed her lantern, shining it over the page. There were six boys and girls, at three different ages. She saw a child, a grown teen, and tucked right in the middle, a pre-teen. The book said the girl in the middle was twelve. Katie was ten – almost eleven – but she shivered as she realized her body was more like the girl at six.

How could this be? How could a life in the woods, a life filled with what the earth provided to her, leave her so small? Katie slipped the book under her pillow and turned off the lantern. She heard her mother and father murmuring in the kitchen. Her parents would make sure she had enough, even when the earth did not. As she went to sleep, she shuddered a little when she realized that thought was a hope as opposed to a certainty.

"Katie, Daphne! I'm back from the wicked place."

Her father grinned as he said the name, and her mother laughed. Katie rolled her eyes. As she neared her teenage years, each year with less food than the last, she only grew to doubt her parents; and this included how true their assessments were of a place that was supposedly bad for her.

"I've just got a few newspapers today," her father said as he lay them down on the table. "Seems a lot of people in the city have been getting sick. They think it's e-coli from the spinach."

"From the bagged spinach, they mean." Her mother rolled her eyes as she leafed through the papers. Scanning them but never reading them. Katie wondered if she ever read them, or if she chose not to so she could keep believing everything she said.

"Well, you know what the wicked dwellers eat. It isn't

real if it isn't in plastic."

"Why do you go into the city if you don't like the people or anything in it?"

Katie's father and mother looked at her in mild shock. "To get a few things we can't get out here," her father said. "Like these newspapers."

Katie folded her arms. She'd been hungry and bitter since she woke up, and both feelings manifested in her words. "You barely read the papers, and even if you did, all they tell you is what you already think: that people suck, and we're better off without them."

"We still need to be informed," her mother said. "The earth gives us food and life, but newspapers and books give us knowledge."

"Oh yeah, I got a couple books, too," her father said. He lifted two green books from the box. "Updated foraging books – at least, as up to date as the used bookstore had."

"Maybe they'll help us find some new food."

"Or maybe we could buy some," Katie said.

Her mother looked up, and her father scowled. "We'd never do that," he said, his voice rumbling under his mustache. "The food we get here is better than anything you'd see in the city."

"At least we'd see something there."

"Yes," her mother said, sharing her father's scowl. "You'd see people dying from the food they eat."

Katie rolled her eyes, which helped distract her parents from her stomach growling. "We don't have to buy spinach. But maybe we could buy some soup, or even some bread –"

"It all comes from the same place. All the food in the city comes from factories, factories that poison the earth instead of sustaining it. That's what makes the food rotten, and why that food gives people cancer or makes them vomit until they die."

Katie's stomach growled. It couldn't discern between cancerous food and sustainable food. It just wanted food.

"The food here isn't exactly helping," Katie said. "Look at me. I'm almost thirteen, and I still look like a kid."

Both her parents furrowed their brows. "What do you mean?" her father asked.

"I actually read the newspapers you bring home. I've seen the pictures in them, and the pictures in all your science books. I still look like a little girl. I'm short …"

"We're not a family of trees," her father said.

"I don't have breasts …"

Her father fidgeted, and her mother said, "Don't worry about your breast size, honey. That's a vanity you don't need."

"And I don't even have my period!"

"I'm going to make dinner," her father said, darting towards the stove. Her mother motioned her towards the bedroom. Katie sat on the bed, and her mother closed the door.

"Katie, why are you concerned about your menses?"

Katie sighed. "I should have it by now. Your science book says so."

"That book is for learning about plants, not your body."

"It teaches both."

"Well, if you looked at more than just the pictures, you'd see that girls typically have their period by twelve or thirteen."

Katie felt an angry, embarrassed burn settle in her heart at her mother thinking she was uninformed.

"You're only thirteen," her mother added. "And some girls get it at fourteen or fifteen."

"And some don't get it at all." Katie looked at her thinning wrists. "I don't think I ever will. I have nothing that the book says a girl my age should have."

"Maybe not by the book." Her mother stroked her back. "But maybe you do by the earth."

Katie stiffened. Her mother's caress ceased.

"What's wrong?" her mother asked.

"What do you mean, by the earth?"

The caress resumed. "Everything you say you don't have – that the book says you don't have – is something related to fertility. Breasts provide milk for babies. Your menses provides blood for an embryo. They set the building blocks for more people." Katie looked up at her mother, who smiled at her. "By not having the means to add more people to the earth, maybe you have everything you need to keep the earth sustained. Everything you need for the earth to keep sustaining you."

Katie wanted to spit. She wanted to jump up, accuse her mother of being ridiculous.

Katie shrugged. "Maybe so."

She knew better than to argue with her mother. She was also too hungry.

Katie couldn't sleep that night. She kept thinking of her mother's words, how her mother smiled as she spoke of Katie not being able to grow. How she'd smiled at her with nothing like kindness.

Mothers were supposed to provide. If one cared for their mother, then one would be sustained. Katie listened to her mother, lived where she said and ate what she and her father offered. She was still hungry.

Her stomach growled so much that she winced. She looked outside and saw the moon was full. It cast a light over her bed that was almost as strong as her lantern. The cabin was quiet. Katie knew her parents were asleep.

She also knew how to ride a bike.

Katie crept outside and hopped on her father's bike. It wobbled a little with the first few peddles, but soon enough, Katie got her bearings and peddled down the worn dirt path connecting their cottage to the city. She wasn't afraid of the dark or the shadows of unknown animals scurrying out of her way. She was too determined to see the lights and buildings she remembered from when she was little. The memories were fading with each day she spent in the woods. She didn't want them to shrivel and die before she did.

The first streetlight nearly blinded her. She blinked and shielded her eyes as the dirt became asphalt and she entered the city. She didn't remember it ever looking like this. Lights dotted the roads, trees, and sidewalks like abscesses. Few people wandered about, but they were there. They walked in small groups or leaned against walls, trying not to be seen in the shadows. One woman leaned against a brick wall with her head in her hands. Katie looked away as the woman knelt down and began to vomit. She figured the woman didn't want to be seen.

Katie remembered a 7-Eleven her father often rode by with a scowl on his way to the recycling center. She rode down the street until she saw its red, green, and white stripes glaring up the road. There was a trash can outside overflowing with wrappers. She felt a rush of hope as she hopped off her bike. Wrappers meant food.

She walked inside and almost buckled over with the light. It reminded her of the way her mother's history books described bombs in far-off places, bombs that destroyed cities in flashes of light. Katie squinted as she meandered through the aisles. She noticed prices underneath the food, and cursed at her lack of money. She hoped the lack of people in the store would help her conceal a few snacks in her pockets to take undetected.

There weren't a lot of people, but they were there. Nocturnal creatures made all the harsher under the fluorescents. She saw men who glowered at cans of beer, women who frowned as they purchased gum. Their faces were gaunt and their fingers were shrunken. Katie felt uncomfortable as she looked at them, and wondered how the city could look so different from what she remembered as a small girl. Her father had said that people in the city were getting sick, but they didn't look sick – they looked close to death. How could the night transform people into monstrous creatures? How could the city cast such a shadow on those who dwelled within it?

Because the city is wicked, and so are the dwellers who live there.

Katie blinked as her mother's voice sounded in her head. She grabbed a few granola bars and focused on her errand. As she walked, she was stopped by a man standing in the aisle. "Hi there," he said.

She looked up. Another gaunt figure, with sunken cheeks and frosty eyes that peaked from beneath bangs the color of straw. He grinned, and Katie could see that his gums were red. He looked down at her chest, even though her breasts were small, as if to remind her that he knew they should be there and he'd leer at her anyway. Katie felt a chill seep from her heart and into her veins.

"Girl like you shouldn't be alone," he said. "So young and so pretty –"

Katie turned away and walked back down the aisle. She ignored the man's footsteps behind her. "You don't need to be alone," he said.

"I'm not alone," she replied as she kept her eyes forward. "I have my parents." And she couldn't wait to return to them, to return to the woods and escape from the wicked place.

"I've been watching you. You're here alone –"

"Get out of my store."

Katie and the man both turned towards the voice. She saw a woman in a red vest grab the man's arm. She had a diamond in her nose, one that glistened under the light. Something beautiful beneath the harshness.

"Leave this girl alone," the woman said. "Go home and take care of yourself."

The man spat on the floor before pivoting to leave. Katie saw that his spit was pink, and that it sat in a small pool of bile. The woman watched him until he disappeared out the door. She looked back down at Katie. Her cheeks were sunken, and parts of her skin were ashen, but she didn't look monstrous. She just looked sick.

"Are your parents sick?" she asked with pity in her voice that Katie didn't understand. Katie didn't know what to say.

"Is that why you're here alone?" the woman continued. "Because they're sick and need food?"

"I need food," Katie said.

"I'm sure you do. Take it. Take what you want." She nodded towards the shelves of granola bars, then swallowed back a retch that crept up her throat. "It doesn't matter anyway," she whispered.

Katie was about to ask what was wrong, what she could do to help the woman. She wondered if the woman could come back to the woods with her, back to where she and her parents were hungry but not ill, in need of food but not in the clutches of the wicked.

Katie's stomach growled, and the woman sighed. "Just take them by the box," she said, before returning to her place behind the register.

Katie placed many boxes in the bin on the back of the bike. Her journey was a little slower from the weight, but it was worth it to get away from the wicked place and return to the woods with food in tow. Katie vowed not to waste it, if only so she wouldn't have to return.

"It's getting harder to go to the wicked place."

Her father walked inside, a stack of papers under his elbow. Katie darted to greet him, having developed a new fondness for the papers after her journey to the city all those months ago. It kept her connected to what was happening beyond their cottage without having to face it herself – and with each passing week, and each repeated headline of deaths and illness beyond the forest, she grew more grateful that she didn't have to face it directly.

"Maybe it's a blessing in disguise," her mother said, kissing his cheek while he handed Katie the latest stack. "It keeps us away from their diseases."

"Maybe so."

Katie couldn't help but agree with her parent's thoughts as she read through the latest deaths in the paper. People were still dying, and in numbers too great to trace to one poisonous crop. "It can't be e-coli, can it?" Katie asked.

"It could be," her father said, as he and her mother

unloaded the remainder of items from his crate. "It could be a multitude of things. Mother Nature has quite the medicine cabinet when it comes to illness."

"Do you think she'll find a cure?"

"I think she already has." Her parents chuckled, and Katie shivered at the sound.

"It's all the better that we're closer to her sources," her mother added. "The closer we are to her, the less likely it is that her food will pass through the hands of man and, with those hands, be scrubbed clean of nourishment."

"And rubbed filthy with death," her father added.

Their words rang true with the food they ate, even with what little they found. The number of people dead grew with each paper her father brought home, people that stayed on the boundaries of the city and within the printed word. Soon, the printed word couldn't contain them. Corpses piled in the city, then past the city and into the country, and further and further until her father's cooking couldn't mask their stink.

"Those damn bodies are poisoning the food," her mother said, her face cross as she stirred a bowl of bark stew. There were no mushrooms that week. "Human rot is seeping into the forest and taking away its ability to provide."

"Even in death, humans are pests," her father agreed, sipping the last of his soup.

"Well, we know what the earth does with pests."

"We're seeing it firsthand."

They chuckled, softer than normal, but no less unsettling to Katie. She didn't chuckle. She didn't protest. She simply sipped her soup. She found it easier to just let her parents be. They were who they were, and they were also her parents. It wasn't her place to fight back or reject them. She knew better than to try. They were there, and Katie left them to themselves, even when she heard her mother vomit later that night.

The woods seemed to hush as more people died. There were fewer plants, and no animals. Katie read in the papers that as people traced the illness to the plants, they began to eat more animals. They forgot that animals ate the plants, forgot that the plants' poison seeped through their flesh even when their hearts stopped beating.

Her parents forgot to bring the papers as they grew more ill. "You go into the wicked place," her mother said one day, her voice a whisper and barely heard over the sound of her father retching. "See what you can find. Just –"

"Follow the path, I know," Katie said. She left out her journey all those years ago, to keep a secret from her mother and to try and bury the fear she had at going back to the wicked place. But her parents needed her to go. They needed her to survive, just as she'd needed them. But neither could save the other from the earth's wrath.

Katie kept a stash of food under her bed, one that only grew in time with her parents' illness. She brought them papers, and books with natural cures, the only kind they would accept. Katie knew the cures were in vain. She watched in despair as her parents wasted away despite their rejection of the city in favor of the earth. The natural had turned against them. There was no cure. There was only time, time which Katie borrowed through snacks and water she consumed in secret.

Even the snacks of man, though, came from the earth's hands. Katie often cried as she nibbled on a granola bar and watched her hands grow no fuller. The food that humans relied on no longer sustained them. The earth twisted its nourishment into one of self-serving, offering food that poisoned the people who poisoned her. Animals too began to die, and so did the flora. Even with her own impending death, Katie couldn't help but feel sorry for a mother who would both poison her children and die herself if it meant she'd no longer suffer.

"Katie."

Her mother's voice flowed through the cottage like a breeze through a cracked window. Katie looked in her direction. Her mother lay on the bed, weak from her last round of vomiting. Her father lay breathless beside her. Her mother lifted a hand, reaching out to her daughter.

Katie walked to her. She sat on the bed and held her mother's sallow hand in her own withering fingers.

"I hope you know," her mother whispered, "that even with all this … even with everything she's taken away …" She looked at Katie's father, then at Katie's hand, then back in Katie's eyes. "… the earth loves you, and does what she does to provide."

Katie kept her gaze and grasp steady. Now wasn't the time to balk at her mother's words, or roll her eyes, or flinch beneath her touch. Her mother was wrong. Her mother being right wouldn't have changed anything. The earth had already decided their fate.

She lifted her mother's hand to her lips and kissed it. Her mother's skin was more delicate than a leaf, and its touch seeped through her senses one last time. "I love you," Katie said.

Her mother stayed still as Katie placed her hand back by her side. She closed her eyes, joining Katie's father.

Katie didn't cry for her parents. She knew she'd join them soon enough. Her stomach no longer growled but mewled in resignation at its empty fate. Even so, she looked under her bed to see if any of her provisions were left. All she saw were wrappers.

Katie moved like a slow-rolling fog through the cottage. She took a paper from the table almost as an afterthought as she went back to her parents. She nestled between them like she'd done sometimes as a girl after having a nightmare. Even cold, their touch gave her comfort from what scared her.

She knew her time was coming. She also knew she had time. She thumbed through one last paper, skipping the headlines on the front page about death tolls, parched cities, doomed civilizations. Katie knew all that without a paper to tell her.

Buried deep within the pages, though, were stories of the mundane – a sense of normalcy amidst the turmoil. Pictures of celebrities – the ones that were still alive, at least – shopping or walking their dogs. Politicians enacting what policies they could before all sense of government was gone. The elderly celebrating milestone birthdays. Katie couldn't help but feel a little better as she read those stories, even when she knew what fate awaited them all.

Katie turned the page and stopped, struck by a full-color photo of yellow wildflowers in a desert. They glowed like beacons in an otherwise barren land. "Desert Born Anew After Years Without Growth," the headline proclaimed. Katie read on about a desert that bore no plants and no life for decades, then was suddenly awash in wildflowers. Park rangers estimated the desert once bore those plants, and now, after years untouched, it had healed itself and started fresh.

Katie sat up. Nature had healed itself. The earth had started fresh. She looked out the window at the barren woods. Perhaps they weren't entirely barren. Perhaps the earth, having started anew, had begun to provide sustenance once more to those who were still there.

Katie was still there – and she was still hungry.

Thus, Katie left her parents in the cottage in search of something to eat. The earth was still there – weakened, and brackish, but there. Katie had to believe that, like the wildflowers in the desert, something lay beyond the choked grass and empty kitchen of their cottage. Something that would nurture her back into life. She sang to herself as she walked, sang the lullabies her mother used to sing to her when she was young. She closed her eyes as she remembered her mother's voice, when it had been stronger all those years ago. It still rang strong in her memories, a strength that seemed to warm her blood and pump her heart.

Katie tripped on a tree branch, and her mother's song stopped short. Her basket skidded away. She stood to retrieve it, then whimpered as she sat back down. She felt too weak to scream. Her knee screamed, clambering for her attention. Food would have to wait.

She examined her knee. It was scraped and bleeding, but not out of use. She looked for grass to wipe the excess blood. All of the blades surrounding her were choked and dried. Her blood gave them more color and moisture than they'd seen in months. She looked at the tree which felled her. The root stood gnarled and black, seeping through the barren grass and oozing from a rotted trunk. Its branches reached into a yellowed sky, like a spider's legs ensnaring a maggot. She remembered how her mother would look at the woods and say in a dreamy voice, "Isn't nature beautiful?" Katie smirked and felt a tiny jolt of strength to heal herself.

Once her knee was dry, Katie stood up and discarded the blades of grass on the ground. She held her hand in front of her after releasing the grass. Her fingers were crooked like the branches above her, and her wrist was gnarled like the roots below. Both poisoned. Both doomed to die. But only one of them had doomed the other.

Katie looked out over the forest – or what was left of it. Decaying trees stretched into the beyond, an army of the dead that marched into eternity. Its branches waited for Katie with open arms. Katie blinked back tears as she looked through the thicket. She knew better than to move forward. The path ahead held nothing but death, a brackish bramble of roots to trip on and bark to disintegrate under her touch.

Katie grew faint and held the tree trunk for support. The bark squished into her palm like a sponge but kept its form long enough to hold her steady. It hadn't yet completely rotted. It hadn't yet lost its ability to nurture her.

She looked once again at the tree's gnarled fingers reaching into the sky. The fingers of the earth, who her mother was convinced would provide. Her mother had been wrong, and yet she'd been right. The earth provided life through death.

Katie wondered if the earth would heal herself once all the pests were gone. She remembered the story of the desert and its wildflowers. If the earth came back, if the forest returned to its green and nourishing state, there would be no people to witness it. The earth would be sure of it.

Katie smiled in spite of herself. It was almost charming, how stubborn the earth could be.

Katie no longer felt stubborn. She didn't feel much of anything, except a desire to sleep. She lowered herself to the ground and leaned against the rotted tree. Its flesh was soft, enveloping her cheek and shoulders as she curled against it. She closed her eyes, and imagined laying against her mother's breast, the gentle breeze of her mother's fingers running through her hair as she sang her a lullaby. Katie whispered in tune with her mother, smiling as she drifted to sleep.

WE REALLY SHOULDN'T

Kelly paced while she waited in line and clutched her laptop bag to her side. She fingered the strap, ran her hands along its surface as she waited to speak through a keyboard. She preferred to speak when cloaked in the safety of typed words and written articles. When she spoke without that cloak, people looked into her – and worse, they spoke back.

Or even worse, they spoke first.

Or worst of all, they spoke against the things she wanted. And when they did that, Kelly wanted to respond with things she shouldn't say. Thoughts she shouldn't have. Words that had no place at all, even in her mind.

"Kelly?"

Kelly looked up. A smiling barista held a white cup in her direction.

"One small coffee for Kelly?"

Kelly managed a perfunctory nod as she took the cup. "Thank you."

She walked towards a table tucked in the corner, away from the hubbub of drinks being steamed and office drones ordering jolts to get through the afternoon slump. A coffee shop wasn't her first choice, but her office was her apartment, and her apartment was being sprayed for bugs.

At least her computer could tell people to stay away in ways that she alone couldn't do. She sipped her drink and opened her laptop, readying her latest blog post. *Should We/Shouldn't We* had been Kelly's pet project for years, a haven for her opinions and the debates she often held in her head. The blog gave her a place to share those thoughts with others – though others often added their own points, whether or not Kelly asked for them.

Still, Kelly wrote. Her next piece was poised to be a good one: a point-counterpoint on whether using public transit encouraged green initiatives or discouraged cities from keeping their character by bringing in too many outsiders. Her fingers ran circles around the keyboard, and her words fell in rhythm with cups being handed to thirsty customers. She paused only to stretch and crack her neck.

A voice in her head reminded her not to focus so much that her neck got stiff. "It puts you out of commission for other things," the voice whispered, hot in her ear as long fingers rubbed her shoulders.

She shook her head and shook off the voice and its fingers. She had work to do.

She took one final sip, and was about to make one final keystroke, when that same voice said, "Kelly?"

Her fingers halted, the cursor beating in time with her heart as it failed to produce a closing sentence. She looked up and saw who she expected to see. Even though it'd been months since she'd heard that voice – outside of her own head, at least – she knew exactly whose it was.

"Josh."

Josh smiled as he walked closer. He looked just like she remembered him – and like he hadn't changed or showered since. He wore a wrinkled white t-shirt, faded jeans rumpled over a pair of dirty boots, stubble grown for an exact number of days, and blond hair oiled brown, as it only ever saw enough shampoo to keep the grease to a minimum.

He always managed to look like a slob – and like always, to Kelly's dismay, he didn't look bad. His faded clothes and lack of grooming did nothing to temper his cedar green eyes or his smile, both of which came dangerously close to her as he stopped in front of her table.

"It's been a long time," Josh said. "How have you been?"

"I've been okay," she replied. She knew better than to give him too many details. "How about you?"

"Can't complain. Mostly doing odd jobs here and there." He cocked his eyebrows at her. "Are you still writing your blog?"

Kelly sighed a little. He always pressed for details – and like always, he managed to get them. "I am," she said. "I'm working on a new post now, actually."

"How about that?" Without asking, he pulled the chair across from her to the side of the table and sat down. "Working on the blog that brought us together."

Kelly couldn't help but smile. She tried to keep it as small as possible to let him know she smiled at the coincidence of it, not the memory. "Your comments were some of my earliest," she said. "Not to mention the most colorful."

"Hey, I liked what I read." Josh leaned on the table, which moved his arm close to hers. A warmth crept across her skin, bridging the gap between them. "And I really liked the author."

"Don't."

His smile fell, and she moved her arm to her lap.

"There's a reason we ended things," she said, her eyes on the monitor. "Please don't remind me why we began them."

"Hey, I'm just sharing a memory." He removed his arm

from the table and folded both hands in his lap. "Even if we're not together anymore, we shared a lot. We always will."

"Always did."

"Yeah, that's what I meant." He gave a half-smile. "Always one to use the right word."

"It matters. The smallest word can change a whole sentence. Sometimes a whole life."

"Like 'goodbye'?"

Her shoulders fell, and she closed her laptop. "Yes. Exactly."

"Josh?"

Josh and Kelly both looked towards the voice. Josh's eyes narrowed at the stranger who'd dare interrupt their exchange. Kelly recognized that look, the glare of animosity towards anyone who spoke to him without his desire. It was one she herself often gave – and one they never gave to each other. She pursed her lips to keep from smiling again.

The barista held another white cup. "Small coffee, for Josh?" The barista gave an extra-wide smile to him, one Kelly knew offered more than just the coffee.

Josh knew, too. He turned on the charm and smiled back as he took the cup. "Thank you," he said as he raised the cup. "Thanks a lot ..." He looked at her nametag, and Kelly saw his eyes take a side trip to her breasts. "Amanda?"

"Mandy," she said with a giggle as she tucked back a strand of her long brown hair. Kelly rolled her eyes. She knew it was an act, that Josh was doing this because she was watching him. She shuddered anyway.

"Thanks, Mandy." Josh nodded, then returned to Kelly. "Well, I was just passing through anyway," he said with a shrug, "so I'll leave you to it."

Kelly nodded back. "It was nice to see you." It was the

truth, as hesitant as she was to admit it.

She should have known better than to admit it out loud. Josh smiled. "Would you like to have coffee tomorrow?" he asked.

Kelly blanched, but didn't say no. He added, "Just to catch up. It's been a long time."

She nodded. "It has." But had it been long enough? She wondered if it would ever be long enough.

"And the fact that I ran into you while you were working on your blog …" Josh smiled. "Well, maybe something's telling us we should reconnect."

"We really shouldn't," Kelly said.

"Even just to catch up?"

"You didn't say catch up. You said reconnect."

He chuckled. "I said both." Kelly rolled her eyes, but with a chuckle of her own. "But if you want to, we can keep it to 'catching up.'"

She shouldn't want to. She knew that catching up would risk reconnecting – something neither of them should do.

She pulled out her phone and opened her calendar. "How about one o'clock?"

Kelly should have been writing. Instead, she was reading, with her legs stretched across the couch and a mug of chamomile tea by her side. All of her old posts were there, collecting dust on the digital shelf as their views stayed stagnant and their comments ceased. Looking through those old comments reminded her of the cruelty that the anonymous mask of the Internet allowed. Trolls peppered her posts with calls to kill herself, show her tits, or get a life. Even the more benign comments irked her, with requests to visit their own websites, misspelled thoughts on her words, or – her least favorite of all – suggestions on what she should say. "I'll say what I want here," she'd mutter aloud as she scrolled through their comments. "In the one place where I can."

Rereading the commenters' words reminded her of how lucky they were to be separated from her ire by a screen. But their words weren't the ones she was looking for. She scrolled and skimmed until she found it – a comment that glowed on the page despite the candle she held for its author having dimmed long ago.

You make an excellent point on knives. A cheesy opening line, but one that caught Kelly's eye, nonetheless. She'd written a post on how frequently one should sharpen their kitchen tools. It wasn't even a question for her. She meticulously sharpened them once a week, wanting no interference as she carved through onion skin and tomato pulp.

However odd it might have been, Kelly felt a strange urge to answer the comment – and find out more about the person who wrote it. They moved from comments to email, from email to phone, and soon, from the phone to a date.

For all of Josh's talk about signs, Kelly wondered how neither of them saw it as one when they bickered on their first date, a cooking class that he'd invited her to. "You're supposed to slice the carrot on the bias," she said, taking the knife from him so she could do it herself.

"You're just supposed to slice it," Josh said with a frown as he placed his hand over the remaining carrots. "It doesn't matter how."

"But it does. It says so right on the recipe."

"As long as they're sliced, the dish will be fine."

"It affects everything: cooking time, evenness, presentation …"

Josh snorted. "Presentation?"

Kelly glared at him. "Yes. It matters."

"Excuse me." Kelly and Josh looked up and saw the instructor stare at them with pursed lips and eyes as thin as the strands of saffron on the counter. "Is there a problem here?"

Kelly and Josh narrowed their eyes, emanating coolness that widened the instructor's stern expression into one of fear. "No," Kelly said, keeping her reply quick in an effort to get the instructor to leave as soon as possible. "We're just having a disagreement."

"Which *we'll* settle," Josh added.

"Please … try to keep it down," the instructor said. Kelly tried not to snicker at the way his voice stammered. "You're bothering the other students."

"Well, you're bothering us," Josh spat. Kelly turned to face him with wide eyes of her own. His gall was surprising – and exactly what she wanted to say. It was a bit of a turn-on.

The instructor regained his composure and set his face once more. "Please leave."

"We will," Josh said, not even asking Kelly if she wanted to leave. He didn't need to. She wanted to go wherever he went.

"What an asshole," Josh said as the door closed behind them.

"Right? We weren't even that loud." She moved towards Josh's body to keep warm as they walked into the cold.

"Fuck him and fuck that class. Let's cook at my place – and slice the carrots any which way, *en bias* or in chunks."

"However, the recipe says," Kelly insisted. He rolled his eyes, and she narrowed hers. "It does matter, Josh."

He smiled and wrapped his arm around her waist. "All that matters to me is cooking with you."

Kelly rolled her eyes again, but with less conviction. She knew she shouldn't be charmed, but even then, she knew that Josh had a way of breaking through her constraints against what she shouldn't do.

The strength of his charm was only so much against the weight of her convictions. "We shouldn't do this anymore," Kelly said as she looked out his living room window. She didn't want his eyes or his smile to bring her back in, the way they had so many times over the past eleven months when she thought of ending things for good.

"Do what?" Josh asked. Kelly closed her eyes so he wouldn't see her roll them. "Make dinner?"

"No." She spun to face him, and her glare was tempered by how sad he looked, something he didn't hide quickly enough. Kelly knew he'd only joked to hide his sadness, but hiding behind jokes was a band-aid on the wound of their relationship.

"I'm serious, Josh," she said, sighing as she looked at the floor. "All we do is argue, and when we try to talk about it, all you do is make jokes."

"There're a lot of other things I do." He moved closer to her and held her arms. "Things we do together."

"Things we shouldn't do together."

"Who cares if we should or shouldn't do them?" He leaned down towards her shoulder. "Just as long as we do them together."

Kelly closed her eyes. The things they did together were

things she never thought of actually doing until she met him. Until he brought the thoughts she'd kept inside up to the surface, and all of them – all of her – breathed for air upon their escape.

Even with Josh, though, a part of her thought that those thoughts shouldn't be there. And they wouldn't be there, if Josh would only leave. And Josh would only leave if he believed that Kelly didn't want to do the things they did.

Kelly knew she couldn't convince him of that. She could, however, convince him of the one thing they did that neither of them liked to do with one another. The one thing that reminded them that they weren't, in fact, one.

"We argue," she said. "Is that okay, as long as we do it together?"

He stopped his descent. She kept her shoulders stiff. He moved his head back up and looked in her eyes. "Do we really argue that much?"

"We're arguing about how much we argue. Shouldn't that tell you everything you need to know about our relationship?"

He smiled a little. "I thought knives did that."

She chuckled, despite herself, at her memories — the comment on her blog, their first date, and the others. Her voice caught as she realized their entire relationship would soon be a memory.

It needed to be. "I can't do this anymore," she said, looking back down at the floor.

"Can't?" he whispered. "Or shouldn't?"

She stayed quiet, and closed her eyes when she felt his lips brush her ear. "The distinction matters," he said.

She refused to be charmed by his focus on wording. "Both."

He sighed against her ear. "If you say so."

She did, and he reluctantly agreed. "You'll always mean something to me," he said as she exited his house.

"You will too," she admitted, pausing in the doorway. "I'll always think of you when I follow a recipe."

He chuckled. "And I'll always think of you when I don't follow directions."

Kelly stayed true to her word, thinking of him whenever she prepared dinner. She'd find herself holding the knife to the side, offering it to a phantom who would help her make the necessary cuts. The ache lessened with each passing month, but like a stubborn stain on a towel run many times through the wash, it never disappeared. It simply faded, living on in Kelly's memory as a closed chapter in her life.

Thanks to her having to work in the coffee shop that day, that chapter hadn't been the end of the book. Kelly set her laptop on the coffee table, then leaned against a pillow and stared at the ceiling. Months had passed, and Josh had only appeared in her dreams and memories. Why had she seen him today? What had brought him to her?

Kelly shook her head. They'd only picked up coffee at the same place, at the same time, and said a quick hello. There was no fate involved. That was Josh's thinking.

She sighed a little as she traced the rim of her teacup. That was Josh's thinking, and only a few hours after he'd been back in her life, she was once again sharing his thoughts.

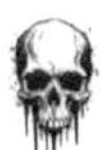

"Josh?"

Josh grabbed their coffee from the barista – thankfully someone other than Mandy – while Kelly grabbed a table. Josh smiled as he took the seat across from her. He'd taken his second shower for the week, but otherwise looked the same as yesterday, save for the stubble growing a little further into a scant blond beard. Kelly tried not to look at his beard, or his lips. Instead, she focused on the coffee cup he scooted towards her. "Just a little milk," he said. "Just the way you like it."

Kelly smiled. "Thank you."

"So." Josh sipped his coffee. "How have you been?"

"You asked me that yesterday. I'm still fine."

"Even with me back in your life?"

"You're in my afternoon, not my life."

"You were always a terrible liar, Kelly. I know I've been in your other afternoons – and not just the ones we spent together."

Kelly looked down to avoid the net cast by Josh seductively raising his eyebrow. "I can lie when it matters – like when I told you how good a job you did cutting up steaks for dinner."

Josh chuckled, and Kelly returned her gaze to him. "I never believed you then, either," he said.

"Did you ever believe anything I said?"

"Yes, but the things I believed are things you don't think we should talk about now."

"I don't. Not really, anyway."

Josh smiled and leaned back in his chair. His chest pushed against the limits of his shirt, and Kelly tried not to notice. She couldn't hold back the memory of running her fingers along its hairs, navigating the golden fields upon his skin and dirtying them with her sweat. She'd trace her fingertips along his heart, and spill secrets as he traced her lips and kissed her shoulder.

"Some of the things we talked about, though …" Josh's

smile grew, and she knew that he was reliving the same memories. She could almost see them running through his head, his thoughts coursing through her as strongly as they had when they were together. Back when they were so close to being one that Kelly had had to sever them back into two.

"Like on our third date," he continued, which snapped her out of her thoughts. He leaned closer to her. Close enough that she felt his breath on her cheek as he spoke. She saw the curls on his chest peek over his collar and curled her fingers under her palm to keep from touching them. "When you told me —"

"Don't."

Josh chuckled a little. "You didn't tell me that. Quite the opposite."

"Maybe it's what I should've said."

"I know you don't believe that." His smile became sly. "Like I said: terrible liar."

Kelly smiled as well, her laugh coming out in a puff that sent the steam of her coffee flying towards him. "You're right," she conceded. "I don't regret saying anything I said to you, or any of the things we shared."

"Do you regret ending them?"

Kelly looked him square in his beautiful eyes. "No."

Josh looked at her for a few moments. His shoulders rose as he took a deep breath. "I wish you were lying," he said at last.

"Like you lied to me yesterday?"

His brow furrowed. "Yesterday?"

"You said you just wanted to catch up. All we've done today is talk about what we had." Kelly's eyes narrowed, her voice growing more cross with each word spoken. "And I know you're talking about that because you want to reconnect, even though you said that wasn't what you meant."

"Well Jesus, Kelly, I can't help it!" He sat back up, his eyes and voice losing all of their cool. "We had something. Something I regret losing every day. And maybe it should've ended when it did. But does that mean we shouldn't start over again now?"

"No," Kelly said, pushing aside her cup. She'd lost all of her thirst. "I should go."

"No, what?"

She furrowed her brow. "What do you mean, 'what?'"

"No, we shouldn't start over?" He stood up, but only to move his chair closer to her. To corner her in. Kelly didn't feel trapped, which scared her more than his maneuvering. "Or no, it doesn't mean we shouldn't?"

Kelly began to protest and instead felt a lump form in her throat. Every memory of their time together was manifesting, reminding her of how much she missed him. How much she shouldn't want what they had together, or what they did together. How much she shouldn't want him – and how much she did anyway.

"I should go," she said again, lifting her purse.

"Should you, or shouldn't you?"

Kelly glared at him, which stopped his smile dead in its tracks. "Don't turn this into a fucking joke, Josh."

"Fine." Josh narrowed his eyes. "Though the real joke is the name of that blog. You know *Should We/Shouldn't We* gives the same answer, right?"

"What the hell do you mean?"

"'Shouldn't We' implies yes. Should we go to the store? *Shouldn't* we go to the store?"

Kelly stood frozen, trapped by a meaning she'd never considered before – and one she couldn't deny was correct.

Josh stood and leaned in close to her, his expression cold. "It's like Will They/Won't They. One is a question of happening. The other's a plea for it to happen."

"Who the fuck cares?" Kelly's exasperation grew harder to hide under the din of the coffee shop's noise. She saw a few people look at them, and longed to get away before they could interfere.

"Neither of them imply opposites." Josh moved closer, close enough to lower his voice. It only landed on Kelly's ears. "Neither of them say no."

She couldn't listen to him anymore, not if she wanted to keep the resolve to do what she should do. "Goodbye, Josh."

He gave a small smile. "That's not no."

"Goodbye." She pursed her lips as she swiveled past him, willing herself to not be drawn in. She sped down the sidewalk as the door slammed behind her. She wove through people heading back to their offices. All ignored her, which was just what she wanted them to do. What they should be doing.

"Kelly!"

Kelly stopped. There was always one who didn't ignore her. There was only one she couldn't ignore.

Josh approached her and slowed when he saw that he had her attention. He stopped a foot away from her. It was still too close. It wasn't close enough.

"I'm sorry," he said.

Kelly closed her eyes. "Thank you."

"I'm sorry for what happened in there." He sighed but stopped when she squeezed his elbow. He closed his eyes, savoring even the smallest of touches.

She removed her hand, and he opened his eyes again. Something told her to end it there. Something smaller told her to stay and say more. Though the desire to stay grew with each beat of her heart, she knew what she should do – even if it wasn't what she wanted.

"Goodbye, Josh." She turned to walk away.

"I found someone."

Kelly stopped.

"Someone else?" she asked.

"Yes." She heard him walk towards her. "Someone new. Just yesterday." His footsteps ceased, and she felt his breath on her neck. "Just after we met."

His fingers landed on her skin. She shuddered at his touch, the chill dissolving into tingles that bled over her skin. They pulsed through her veins and breathed new life into her bones.

"Do you like her?"

"Yes." His body joined his fingers against her skin. "But things aren't the same without you," he said.

"Aren't they?"

She felt him smile against her ear, and she chuckled a little as he gave her a kiss. "Come home with me," he whispered.

She leaned against him, sighing as his lips moved down to her neck. "I shouldn't," she said, with barely a quarter of her heart.

He turned her around, pressing his forehead against hers as he traced her cheek. "Shouldn't you?"

Kelly felt invigorated as they rode to Josh's place, kissing him the way she had when they were together. They were together now. They had to be. To banish him was to banish her. They needed each other. They needed to do the things they shouldn't do. It was the only way they could survive. She curled her fingers under his shirt collar, holding the fabric tight as the hairs beneath it tickled her knuckles. She didn't care if the Uber driver could see. She only cared about being near Josh again.

"We're here."

Kelly and Josh separated and saw the driver giving them a pointed look. Josh smiled all the same. "Thanks," he said, giving a quick wave. The driver furrowed her brow, and Kelly giggled as they exited the car and sped to Josh's house.

Josh pulled her to him as soon as the door closed. He ran his hands up and down her waist, ran his lips up and down her neck. "I missed you so much," he whispered, his breath hot on her ear. He pressed against her and began to lift her shirt.

"Where is she?"

Josh dropped her shirt and looked into her eyes. "She?" he asked. "There's only us." He began to kiss her neck. "That's all there ever is."

"Don't lie to me." Kelly pushed him away, then began to run her palms over his body, softening him up to loosen his words. "I know she's here."

He smiled. "You know me too well."

"I should, after all we've shared." She kissed him and gently bit his lip as she pulled away. "Where is she?"

He kissed her back, then moved his lips to her earlobe and gave it a gentle nip. "If you know me so well," he whispered, "then you should know exactly where she is."

"Tell me a secret."

Kelly and Josh lay on his bed, an empty bottle of wine

on his bed stand. She'd spent the better part of the past hour licking wine from his lips, sighing as they spoke in whispers and touched each other with tongues and fingertips alike. It was only their third date, and Kelly already felt so close to him, as if the only thing between them was a layer of skin and a body containing their entwined souls.

"Any secret?" she asked.

"Any of yours."

Kelly laughed as he kissed her neck. It was only their third date, and already she couldn't fool Josh with her words. "What if I don't have any?"

He looked up at her with a bemused grin. "I know you have them." He traced his finger along her cheek. "And I know you're dying to share them with someone."

She closed her eyes. "Maybe they shouldn't be told."

"Maybe you should tell them to me." He kissed her lips, which broke into a small smile. "Maybe I share them."

He couldn't know that, but something told her that maybe, just maybe, he did. She kissed him and began to whisper. "I love it when it's us," she said.

"That's not a secret," he whispered as kissed her back.

"I hate it when we're interrupted," she continued.

"Like that asshole at the cooking class?"

"Like anyone. By people on the street, by waiters interrupting us when we just want to eat … I hate it when they're there. And I love it when we disappear together and cut them out of our lives."

"I love that too." He pulled down her panties, kissing a line from her shoulder to her stomach. Kelly gasped upon his touch, upon the possibilities that the two of them together could realize.

"But maybe if we brought them in together … maybe it

wouldn't be so bad."

He paused and looked up at her. "Brought them here?" he asked. "With us?"

"Yes. With both of us."

He smiled and moved his fingers up her side as he returned to her neck. "I'd like that," he said as he kissed her neck. "I'd like that a lot."

"I would too." She pulled him close and kissed his chin. The stubble scratched her, and she relished the thought of licking her chapped lips the next morning. "Especially when we get rid of them after."

Josh didn't pause. He rolled on top of her, and Kelly felt his growing erection. "As we should," he whispered.

Kelly moaned as he slid between her legs. "As we will."

"Josh?"

Kelly narrowed her eyes. She recognized that voice. It had called their names before. "Seriously, Josh?" she said. "The fucking barista?"

Josh shrugged, and a devious grin crossed his face. "She was cute."

Kelly rolled her eyes. "You always went for the easy ones."

"What does it matter?" He gestured towards his bedroom door. "As long as they end up here."

Kelly smiled a little as she walked through the door and saw the barista on the bed. "Yes. Exactly."

"Who is that?" The barista looked from right to left, despite the blindfold obstructing her view.

"It's Kelly, Mandy," Josh said. "Don't you remember from yesterday?"

"What's going on?" Mandy asked as she moved her head back to the right. It was all she could do, since her wrists and ankles were handcuffed to the bedposts.

Josh walked towards her and traced his fingers along her chin. Mandy shuddered upon his touch. He removed the blindfold, revealing frantic eyes underneath. They sped from Josh to Kelly, a stray tear racing down her chin. "Did he get you too?" she asked, looking up at Kelly.

Kelly laughed at Mandy's mistake and smiled when she saw that her laughter scared Mandy more. "I did," Josh said, a smile settling on his lips as he looked at Kelly. "And I couldn't be happier."

Kelly smiled back at him. "Neither could I."

"Please let me go." They turned their attention back to Mandy, who bit her lip to keep from crying. "I won't tell the cops. I won't even tell my friends. Just let me go."

Josh stroked his beard, and Kelly bit her own lip to keep from laughing again. "Maybe we should," he mused. He walked towards the bed and touched the keys on the bedside table. The woman's eyes widened further, hesitant delight flickering in her irises.

Josh moved his hand. "But maybe we shouldn't." Kelly grinned as she saw his fingers float down to the drawer. He opened it and brought forth his largest knife. Kelly's eyes lit up, while Mandy's widened in fear. Josh held it out as he walked back to Kelly. She lowered his hand so she could kiss him without getting cut. Her lips met his, and she held him as close as she could, vowing to keep them as one.

"Let me go!"

They stopped. Josh pulled away and turned to face

Mandy. Kelly narrowed her eyes. She and Josh weren't one – not with someone else around. Not with all the others they avoided together, then decided together to take care of themselves. To sever them from their existence, breaking the others back into two – or four, or even ten, depending on Kelly's mood.

Josh smiled again, and looked at Kelly, raising his eyebrow as he held up the knife. "Should we?"

Kelly smirked and took the knife from his hand. "Shouldn't we?"

"Please, Kelly." Mandy's lip trembled as the anger in her eyes flickered away. Scared resignation took its place, and Kelly almost felt sorry for her. "Please let me go," she whimpered.

Kelly walked towards Mandy and knelt by her side. "I should," she said. She ran her fingers through Mandy's hair. Sweat slicked Kelly's palms as she gave Mandy a gentle caress.

Mandy closed her eyes. Took a breath.

Kelly grabbed Mandy's hair. She yanked back her head, and Mandy's eyes snapped open as Kelly placed the blade against her throat. "But I won't."

WEARY BONES

Brandon sipped his beer as he watched TV. Occasionally, a gust of rain splashed against his house like water crashing from a thrown bucket; otherwise, he paid no attention to the storm outside. He'd had a long day, one spent dusting and cleaning and tending to his wards. They were all asleep — as asleep as they could be — and now, he had an evening to himself.

He chose to spend that evening with *Law and Order: SVU.* Olivia Benson had long retired, and her great-granddaughter, Tiffany Benson-Sweet, had taken up the mantle of investigation. But through all the seasons and all the Bensons, Brandon still found the show to be a comfort after a long day at work.

His doorbell rang, a single chime that sounded over the television. Brandon sighed as he set down his mug and turned off the TV. So much for an evening to himself. He stood up and winced at his aching knees. He frowned at the sheets of rain unfurling outside of his window. Who would come to see him in this weather?

Brandon opened the door. A skeleton stood on his porch. It stood upright, its hollow eyes staring into Brandon's face. Rain ran down its skull and fell in droplets off of its ribs. Its teeth were clenched, and its arms hung slack by its sides.

Brandon nodded towards the living room. "Come on in," he said.

It started with a serum to ease the pain of death. It didn't prevent death but promised a second life to people when their bodies stopped working. "Eventually, we hope to have a serum that gives people as many lives as cats," its inventor quipped on TV.

Dr. Soo Lin McCarthy watched the press conference from her lab and chewed on her fingernail. She wasn't as excited as her colleagues, for she knew what they meant by a second life. If it had been up to her, they wouldn't be presenting the serum at all. But it wasn't up to her, something their managers made clear despite the rattling in the rats' cages that could be heard even through closed doors. "It'll be fine once we get it to human testing," her managers assured her.

Soo Lin wasn't involved with human testing, but she gathered from the active silence about the effects of the serum that it hadn't been much better for them than it had been for the rats. She shuddered at the memory as the televised press conference continued and the serum's inventor announced patients would soon be able to request it at all medical offices.

She could still hear the sound of bone against metal, a clanking that had sounded like marbles spilling or dice rolling whenever she opened the door. She could still see the rats' eyeless faces staring at her, hungry for food they couldn't eat. She could still feel the sickness in her stomach that grew with every crunch she'd heard when her bosses ordered the rats to be destroyed.

Soo Lin bit through her fingernail, then spit the nail into the trash. She turned off the TV and got her coat. People would find out soon enough how good the serum's promise was.

Brandon didn't remember the promises of the doctors or the excitement in the papers. He barely remembered the pain of the serum. He'd received it when he was three, and all he remembered was the cool seat beneath his legs and the white walls he studied while a nurse promised him a lollipop.

What he remembered more was seeing his grandfather die. His grandfather was able to stay at home because of the serum, although he was bedridden in Brandon's earliest memories. On the night he took a turn for the worse, everyone gathered in his grandfather's room. Brandon stood restless next to his mother and watched as his father stared at Brandon's grandfather. His Aunt Maria sobbed in the corner, and his Uncle Leo patted her shoulder. "He's going to come back," Leo said assuringly. "You don't have to cry."

"It's still sad," Brandon's father said with a frown, one Brandon usually saw when he spilled his cereal or told his father no. "She's allowed to grieve."

"And I'm allowed to comfort my wife," Leo shot back.

"Do you really need to do this now?" his mother snapped, as Aunt Maria cried harder.

They were all silenced by a deep, sudden breath. The family looked at the bed. Brandon's grandfather didn't move.

"Dad?" Brandon's father stepped toward his grandfather. Aunt Maria wiped her tears and leaned forward. Brandon still remembered the way his mother's fingers pressed into his shoulders as Brandon's father took his grandfather's hand.

"No pulse," his father said.

"How long does it take?" Aunt Maria asked.

"Do they have a pulse when they come back?" Uncle Leo added.

"Leo," Aunt Maria warned.

"What? I'm just wondering."

"Shit!"

Everyone looked at Brandon's father as he jumped back. His palm appeared to be melting, but Brandon realized the blood, ooze, and skin weren't his. They were his grandfather's. Brandon stood on tiptoe and watched in awe as his grandfather's body rippled and dripped, the skin dissolving and the blood congealing into the organs. His lungs, stomach, and other parts that Brandon didn't know the names of all began to beat like his heart. They beat as they dissolved, vanishing into the pool of bodily sludge that seeped into the sheets.

Aunt Maria screamed, while Uncle Leo turned to vomit into a small trashcan. Brandon's mother spun him out of the room just as his grandfather's heart faded into his ribs.

Meanwhile, in a small town almost a hundred miles away, Penny Pinkerton unknowingly thrust atop a dead man. "Come on, Glenn," she said as she lifted his hands to her hips. "Put some effort into it." She arched her back and jutted out her breasts, which she knew he loved and always responded to.

Glenn's hands slid down her waist. Penny opened her eyes and saw him lying still beneath her. He wasn't breathing, despite their chosen activity for the evening.

Penny slid off of him. It was his heart, maybe, or a stroke, or some other health problem that hadn't come up between them during any of their weekly visits at the Super 8. She wasn't about to spend a lot of time finding out. That would be for his wife to deal with.

The staff could also deal with moving the body. Penny covered Glenn with the comforter, then grabbed her coat from the chair and put it on over her pink lingerie. There was no point getting dressed at this hour, not even for the long drive in the cold back to her apartment. She'd been looking forward to a warm evening with Glenn.

She glanced back at the bed. Glenn was now a body under a blanket – a dirty hotel blanket at that. Penny could've sworn the stains that were already on it had grown since she'd covered him. The hotel's smell was also starting to get to her now that sex wasn't distracting her senses. Penny turned away with a sneer and walked towards the phone. It was time to do her part and get out.

"Hi," a lazy voice answered when she called the front desk. "How can I help you?"

Penny was about to say, "The man I'm with has died." But upon thinking the phrase, a lump formed in her throat. Glenn was dead. She wouldn't see him anymore, wouldn't be able to call him when she felt lonely, wouldn't drive to the Super 8 each Friday night and enjoy his company. Glenn was gone.

"Hello?" the front desk assistant asked.

"Hi. Yes." Penny spoke as well as she could with a choked voice.

"How can I help you?"

Penny took a deep breath. She refused to be sentimental about Glenn. She'd miss him, but he'd never been hers. He certainly wouldn't be now. She closed her eyes and allowed herself a few final memories, like how his lips had grazed her chin and how his palms had held her waist. She swore she felt his fingers touch her cheek.

A scratch along her ear broke her thoughts. She turned around and was face-to-face with a skull. A bony hand caressed her cheek.

Penny's scream sounded loud and clear through the phone.

Brandon's grandfather stayed in their house, despite the lingering fright from the transformation on his death bed. Whenever his grandfather walked from room to room, the creak of his bones sounding through the halls, Brandon's parents would exchange a wary glance.

Brandon, however, didn't mind. While his grandfather couldn't do everything he'd done before, like tell him bedtime stories or hold Brandon in his lap (he'd tried, but Brandon complained about the bumps on his butt), they could still play games or sit on the porch and watch the sunset.

Brandon especially loved playing games with dice. He liked the sound of the dice rattling in his grandfather's palms. His grandfather noticed and always made sure to take his turn with extra flourish. He'd sometimes hold the dice up to his empty eye sockets, which always made Brandon laugh.

"How long can we keep a skeleton in the house, though?"

Brandon's parents spoke behind him while he watched TV, convinced he wasn't listening. His grandfather had already gone to bed. "It's been over a year," his father continued. "I loved Dad — I love Dad — but it's not Dad. It's just his bones."

"It is Grandpa," Brandon said as he turned around. "He

plays with me and watches TV and —"

"It's a memory of Grandpa," his mother said.

"No, it's him! If it wasn't him, then why would he be moving around and playing games and —"

"It's not the same," his dad said. "And there's more to think about than keeping Grandpa's memory around the house."

"He's not a memory!" Brandon jumped up and stormed out of the room before his parents could say more. He ran up the stairs, then slowed his pace as he approached his grandfather's door. He almost felt a coolness coming from the other side of the door, like the feel of an autumn walk.

Brandon opened the door and saw his grandfather propped up in bed, reading a newspaper. Brandon wondered how he could still read, even without eyes. Maybe something in the serum brought back memories of words or let him see through sockets instead of eyeballs.

His grandfather looked up at him. He waved and patted the mattress, turning the paper to reveal the comics. Brandon smiled as he joined his grandfather, who put an arm around Brandon's shoulders. Brandon read the panels out loud and barely noticed the feel of bone against his back. He did see a white, dusty film across the pages, streaks left with every flick of his grandfather's fingers. Brandon's heart grew heavy as he realized his grandfather, like bones in a cemetery, would turn to dust. But they could read together before that happened.

It'd been hard enough for Marion to watch her child slowly die from cancer. Cecily had spent the last two years of her life in and out of the hospital. Tubes and beeping machines had become as prominent in Marion's memory as Cecily happily banging on the dashboard during drives, or the soft sound of her cries when she'd had a nightmare. Cecily was too young to be so sick, their time together too short. Cecily would never have a first day of school. She'd barely had a life outside of diapers. Even after the effects of the serum had become well known, Marion thought having her daughter back in some capacity would give them both the life together the disease had stolen from them.

Cecily had died at home, per Marion's request. She'd left Cecily sleeping in her bed and closed the door behind her so she wouldn't have to see the transformation. She'd already laid down a rubber sheet to catch the blood. As she waited in her room, she imagined hearing Cecily's cries once more, the whimper that meant Cecily would soon be crawling into bed with her after a nightmare.

Marion waited, then waited some more. Her eyes grew heavy, but she was startled awake by a loud rattle. It jangled and clanged down the hall, the sound of bone against a wooden door. Her daughter was back — but Marion felt a sickness in her stomach at the sound of bones.

She shook her head. Cecily was alive, and that was what mattered. She rose to her feet to go hug her daughter.

Marion could not grow used to the feel of Cecily's skeleton in her arms. Cecily longed to be held, longed to eat her favorite cereal and to play with Barbies. She could eat the cereal (though Marion refused to add milk), but Marion could barely eat as she watched Cecily's Lucky Charms fall down her rib cage. She'd play with Cecily and her Barbies, but Marion could only see a skeleton braiding Barbie's hair.

Looking at Cecily's skeleton reminded Marion of her death every time. Marion remembered the tubes, the beeps, the shallow breaths and endless rounds of vomiting. She remembered holding her daughter's hand in the hospital, her skin weak and her bones showing through more with each passing week.

Marion cried every night after Cecily crawled into bed. She thought the serum would give them both a second life. Cecily lived, but Marion perpetually grieved, reminded every day of the daughter she'd lost.

Marion first saw a commercial for the living cemeteries as she watched TV through teary eyes. Many people couldn't cope with the living memento mori of their loved ones, so cemeteries were now being used to house the skeletons. Caretakers watched them, and they were surrounded by other skeletons and the people who visited them.

She'd dismissed the notion, but with each passing day, she wasn't sure if she herself could live, so long as Cecily's bones clattered through the halls. She'd forever be in mourning, even when Cecily became nothing but dust. Skeletons were supposed to disappear in graveyards. Only memories were supposed to fade in houses.

They went for one last drive together. Marion fastened Cecily's seat belt, careful not to press the belt too tight against her ribs. Cecily banged on the dashboard like she had as a girl. Marion tried not to tense at the sound of bone hitting vinyl. "Stop, honey," Marion said as she gently took Cecily's hand.

Cecily stopped and curled her fingers around her mother's palm. Marion blinked back tears, but not at the feel of bone. For the rest of their drive to the cemetery, all she felt was the warm skin of her daughter's hand.

Brandon didn't mind the living cemeteries at all. He often waved at the skeletons when he walked by on his way to and from school. Sometimes they waved back. Other times, they nodded in his direction.

Most passersby turned their heads, but Brandon wasn't the only one who waved. There were others like him who didn't mind the bones, who saw them as a regular part of their lives, not creepy reminders of the people they'd lost.

Whatever one's thoughts on the bones, there were more and more of them every day — and with more skeletons came more crowding, more grime, and more concern. People may have been uncomfortable keeping their loved ones in their home, but they didn't want their loved ones' care to fall to the wayside.

As such, their care within the living cemeteries became a bigger priority. As Brandon walked by the cemetery on his usual route, he saw a flyer taped to the iron gate:

Help Wanted: Caretaker(s) to help with skeletons. Tasks: clean dirt and grass from bones, clean grave beds, interact with residents, etc.

Brandon thought of his grandfather, who'd perished long before the living cemeteries were in place. His bones had worn to shells that Brandon had feared would become ash at any moment. They sat on the porch, and Brandon noticed his grandfather hadn't moved in some time. When he studied his grandfather, he swore he saw contentment deep within the hollow of his face — a contentment Brandon felt surely came from not being alone when he'd passed.

It was nothing like the feeling he got when he walked by the cemetery. Clustered together, the skeletons emanated waves of sadness that Brandon could feel. They were being forgotten while the living moved on.

These skeletons were alone. Even clustered against one another in cemeteries and seen by friends and family who dared to visit them, they slept and woke up alone. They were left to wither away above ground. Brandon couldn't stop them from withering, but he could lessen their loneliness during the process.

"Can I help you, young man?" Brandon looked up and saw an older woman approach the gate. "You here to visit someone, or —"

"I'm reading about the caretakers," Brandon said. "Do you hire high schoolers?"

Mandy hated walking home after work. The route was safe, and there was never any trouble. The sidewalks were awash in light from the streetlamps, and the empty office buildings lining them shimmered with lit windows. Still, she walked down the sidewalk wary of the darkened corners, head up high and hands in her pockets.

What creeped her out the most was the living cemetery. It'd been creepy enough when it was just a regular cemetery, silent graves that seemed to watch her as she passed by. It got worse when all the skeletons were crowded into it. Most were still when she walked by them, resting in some form of sleep. How did they sleep? Did they just turn off when the sun went down?

However they did it, they creeped Mandy the hell out. She braced herself as she rounded the corner, prepared for the view of a sea of bones lined up one-by-one, the path of ribs almost creating a wave that rippled through the night.

She was greeted by an empty cemetery, filled only with stones.

Mandy stopped and stared. Where had the skeletons gone? Were the caretakers cleaning them? Had they been moved somewhere out of sight?

For the sake of her nightly walk, Mandy hoped they'd been moved. She continued past the graveyard and moved down the sidewalk. The wind was cold on her cheeks. She wanted to get home, change out of her waitressing uniform, and have a cup of tea.

A loud, sickening crack burst behind her. Mandy jumped, then turned around. She saw no one there, no broken trees or shattered rock.

She looked down and saw a pile of bones at her feet. A skull lay on a bed of broken ribs and femurs. Its mouth and eyes gaped up at her, seeming to ask questions in response to her own.

Another crack sounded behind her. Mandy swiveled and saw another pile of bones, this one splayed in a line from the skeleton's shattered toes to its fractured head. "What the fuck?" Mandy whispered.

In answer, a skeleton fell from the sky a little further down the sidewalk. She watched it explode, its bones careening to all sides like shrapnel. She stepped back and felt a crunch beneath her feet. She saw a broken hand beneath her shoe, and felt a little nausea replace the fear that had settled in her stomach.

The sound of cracks came faster now, and on both sides of the street. Mandy looked up.

Skeletons lined the rooftops of the adjacent buildings. One by one, they jumped from the roofs and shattered on the sidewalks, their bones scattering across the pavement and concrete. Mandy ran into the middle of the street, moving as fast as she could so she wouldn't be hit. Her vomit landed on the pavement when she opened her mouth to scream.

So many were dead. If they weren't in pieces on the street, they had buried themselves under mud and sand, waiting for the water to wash them away more quickly than air ever could. Brandon scowled as he picked wet leaves off the skull of one of the only survivors of the Second Death, as the papers called the sudden rash of skeletons ending their reincarnation earlier than science intended.

It was all so unnecessary. It'd been over twenty years since the serum was introduced. The second chance at life was a part of everyone's life. So many people had gotten the serum that, even when it went off the market, people knew there would be skeletons for decades.

Why couldn't they accept that? Why did they have to shudder at the sight of the future that lay ahead for them all? Why did they have to shove those who lived again into places of the dead, like cemeteries and morgues? They were meant to hold those who were gone, those who couldn't feel or see. Those who would fade into the earth the same way they'd fade in their loved ones' memories.

"It's all so fucked up," Brandon said.

He'd spoken to himself, but the skeleton he tended to nodded. Brandon smiled.

"You don't like it here, do you?" Brandon asked.

The skeleton lifted its shoulder bones towards its chin in a makeshift shrug. There was a clatter when the shoulder bones dropped, as if its body rang with the defeat it felt at not knowing the answer.

"Where would you live — you know, if you could?"

Brandon realized he needed to think of a way to phrase the question as yes-or-no, but the skeleton turned before he could. The skeleton gathered some twigs and branches off the ground and wrote, in broken but discernible letters, *HOUSE*.

Brandon nodded. A house would be nice. So many houses, though, were owned by people who didn't want skeletons inside of them. If more people were like him and the other caretakers, perhaps the skeletons would have a home.

Brandon thought for a moment. Why couldn't he and the other caretakers bring the skeletons home? They'd be protected from the elements, and with people who weren't afraid of them. They could live out their lives, if not at home, then at least in a house with creature comforts. They would no longer be surrounded by the terrified eyes of passersby or reminders that they were still considered dead. They wouldn't feel compelled to jump, be buried, or be washed away. They would be home.

So, Brandon took them home.

Emily still thought of him sometimes. She thought of the way his brown hair hung in his face while he wiped dirt and leaves from a skull, how his clothes were often covered in bone dust, and he'd wipe them from his jacket like a baker brushing flour from an apron. "Careful with the dust," she said one day. "I don't want to sneeze out someone's mother."

He'd looked up in surprise, and when he saw Emily's

smile, he'd smiled as well. She held out her hand. "I'm Emily," she said. "I just started working in this cemetery."

"Brandon," he said as he shook her hand. "I've been working here for over five years."

"Wow. Guess this isn't part time for you, huh?"

"Not anymore. Why? Is this a summer job for you?"

The way Brandon's brow furrowed in spite of his smile should've told Emily that unless she saw a future in the graveyard, she'd have no future with him. In that moment, though, Emily only saw beautiful hazel eyes that held secrets. She wanted to uncover those secrets.

"At the moment, yeah," she replied. "Can't do full-time while I'm in school."

"High school?" Brandon asked.

"College."

He nodded and brushed back his bangs, a movement whose magic Emily couldn't deny. "Well, let me know if you need any help," he said as he turned to leave. "I'm here almost every day."

"Even on weekends?" Emily asked. "You don't go out for dinner or anything?"

She grinned and hoped he'd take the hint, but Brandon only shook his head.

"The work doesn't end," he said. "I'm here every day."

He left. Emily shrugged. "I mean, everyone's gotta eat," she muttered as she stooped to clean the hands of a skeleton with moss and dirt on its fingers.

The skeleton nodded, then placed its palm against its forehead before pointing in Brandon's direction. Emily chuckled a little. "Maybe he'd go if you told him to," she said.

Though he didn't seem interested in dinner, Brandon did seem more interested in her the longer she worked at the cemetery. He often worked close to her assigned corners and offered to do her rounds with her when he wasn't busy. Emily felt her fleeting attraction root into something more palpable each day. She hoped and searched for hints in his eyes or his smile that his thoughts had shifted from his work to her.

As weeks turned to months, and months into years, Emily knew that things between them would always be the same. Brandon wasn't interested. Emily was second to the dead.

She left her work in the cemetery upon graduation. She and Brandon promised to keep in touch, but she knew they never would.

When the Second Death occurred, she thought momentarily of the skeletons she'd cared for years ago. Mostly, though, she thought of Brandon. She thought of the way he cared for the skeletons as if they were all his deceased relatives. She thought of how he was probably mourning them, these skeletons who'd decided that total death was better than a partial life. She went to sleep that night hoping that he had someone who could comfort him.

Brandon's house became a destination for the local dead. He heard word of other caretakers following his example, but there were days when Brandon saw all the bones in his house and doubted that.

The other caretakers didn't matter, though. What mattered to Brandon was helping them. His grandfather had died with family both times. When his own parents died, they could come live with him too.

It was possible that it would be the only way he'd see

them. They constantly asked Brandon to come see them but wouldn't visit him. His mother still shuddered when she spoke of the bones. His father avoided the subject. His own mother and father were just like everyone else, the family, friends, and lovers who withdrew from him as his job expanded and his calling came through like a song.

Brandon spent more time at home, and more time with the skeletons and his television for company. If people didn't want to see the memento mori he cared for, the skeletons who just wanted some sort of connection to the life they'd been promised by the serum, then that meant they wouldn't see him either.

The years went by. The skeletons became his life — and for Brandon at least, it was a life well-lived.

Emily moved on in most every sense. She married, she had children and grandchildren. She grew old and spent her afternoons on the porch looking out at the sky. She didn't know when death would come for her, but she was slightly comforted by the thought that when it came, that would be the end. She'd been born after the serum had revealed itself to everyone and never received it. She wouldn't become a walking reminder that she had already died, ignored or avoided by those who wouldn't, or couldn't, mourn the dead among them forever. Those who weren't like Brandon.

She hadn't thought of his name in years, and yet when it flickered in her mind, she saw him standing in the graveyard brushing dirt and bone dust from his palms. She wondered if he was alone. She wondered if he'd turned into one of his beloved skeletons. Did he still care for them as they dwindled in number, the cemeteries once again becoming places for bodies, and the memories they carried, to be buried in the ground?

Emily looked at her wrinkled hands. They'd grown so thin that one could almost see the bones inside of them. She smiled a little as she took in her skeletal appearance. Maybe now, Brandon would be willing to hold her hand.

"Do you want a cup of coffee?"

In lieu of furrowing its absent brow, the skeleton pointed to its throat and then the gaps in its ribs.

"I know," Brandon said. "It was a joke — granted, not a very good one."

The skeleton stood still. Brandon sighed a little. He turned away, then heard a faint rattle. He looked back at the skeleton. It nodded its head and opened its mouth, so it looked more like it had a smile. Its hands were on its ribs, which shook up and down. The bones rattled, and in their clacking, Brandon could almost hear the *ha ha ha.*

Brandon chuckled and turned back toward the kitchen.

"Well, feel free to have a seat," he said as he walked to the stove. "I'm just going to have another cup, and then —"

A violent pang shot up his leg. Brandon swiveled and grabbed his knee, but the turn sent him spiraling. As he fell towards the hard linoleum floor, Brandon wondered what it was like for his wards, who saw and heard and felt despite their lack of bodies. Were their senses like memories, flickers in their skull that helped them move through the next phase of life? He supposed he was about to find out.

Brandon's back fell against a hard bar, one that splintered beneath him. Brandon felt fingers grip his waist. The bar pushed him upward, and Brandon realized that it was a bone.

The skeleton had broken his fall. The skeleton had saved him from death — or at the very least, a score of fractures and breaks that would've rendered Brandon immobile.

The skeleton cradled him as it helped him to his feet. It used both hands to steady Brandon before gently lifting its fingers away to see if Brandon could stand. He stood still and stared into the skeleton's hollow eyes. He stared death in the face — and yet, this death that others avoided while they were alive had kept him living for a while longer.

"Thank you," Brandon said.

The skeleton gave a single nod.

"Come on — I'll get you to an empty room." Brandon nodded towards the stairs. Though he was careful to not move too fast, he walked delicately to ease his aching knees and, now, his sore legs and hip. He trembled—just a little, but enough for the skeleton to wrap its arm around his waist. Brandon was about to shake it off but stopped. He allowed his weary body to be guided by weary bones, both of them ready to rest.

HEARTS ARE JUST "LIKES"

Hailey's fingers trembled as she steadied her phone. It was always difficult to get her best side just right, but when she did, the result was beautiful. Her dimple appeared, her freckles sparkled, and her hair fell in a way that accented her eyes.

Of course, there were filters and Photoshop, but Hailey liked to keep her selfies as real as possible. Being real was what made her so popular online. Being real was what got her a like from Kim Kardashian when Hailey posted a photo of herself spritzing on Kim's new perfume and tagged her. Being real made thousands of strangers flock to her account to fill her feed with likes and led hundreds of companies to offer her samples of their own perfumes, or their foods, or their lotions, or whatever Hailey could promote on their behalf by being a real face for their real product.

Hailey had a job to do on Instagram, a job that brought in likes and money. She'd do anything to keep it. Fortunately, all she had to do was take her picture.

Before snapping her latest selfie, Hailey angled the camera a little more to the left. She didn't want the splash of blood on the wall to be visible. She smiled, then took her picture. It had 3,000 likes within two minutes.

Hailey had many admirers who posted compliments, both kind and lewd, on her feed. TommyBoy89 was one she'd noticed amidst the din of all the rest. TommyBoy89 showered her with hearts and liked every single one of her posts. It wasn't long before she noticed his photo next to his likes. She clicked through to his profile and saw a pair of beautiful eyes looking into hers, and a smile that was just as lovely.

Hailey liked his latest picture and added a comment: *You like so many of my pics. Why don't you say hi?*

TommyBoy89 didn't respond. Hailey shrugged and forgot about her comment until the next day, when she posted a selfie with a tamarind bubble tea from a new café in Georgetown — complimentary, of course, so long as she tagged the café and added #yum in addition to #ad.

TommyBoy89 liked her photo within three minutes — and shortly after, he added a comment: *Hi.*

Hailey followed him and immediately sent a direct message so they could talk in private. They introduced themselves and found out the basics: they both lived in DC, they both spent a lot of time on social media, they were the same age and liked the same restaurants. It didn't take long to meet at an Italian place they both liked, and because the small talk was out of the way, it didn't take long for Hailey to invite TommyBoy89 — who had asked her to call him Tom — to her apartment, where they spent the rest of the night and the better part of the morning having sex.

They became a couple and began to post online together. Tom had a bit of a following himself — not quite as large as Hailey's, but large enough to where they could be considered an Instagram power couple. Hailey's selfies were interspersed with pictures of Tom looking over her shoulder, and her comments were frequently littered with starry-eyed followers declaring the two of them to be #relationshipgoals.

Hailey wondered if they'd feel the same if they noticed that Tom's likes had disappeared in time with them becoming close. After they'd been together for almost six months, her likes — and subsequent offers from companies to promote their products and enhance her brand — continued to skyrocket. However, none of those likes had come from TommyBoy89.

"Why aren't you liking my pictures anymore?" Hailey asked one day as they sat sprawled on her couch.

"I'm in a bunch of them," Tom answered as he scrolled through Instagram. "I feel weird liking my own face."

"There are plenty without you."

"I can tell you I like them in person." He leaned forward and kissed her cheek. "I like how your hair looks today, and those coconut pancakes you made this morning were delicious."

Hailey smiled, but didn't laugh. "I miss your hearts though," she said with a pout that was only somewhat fake.

"Hearts are just likes." Tom kissed her temple. "And I don't just like you. I love you."

"I love you, too." But her answer was distant, her thoughts lost in her feed as she scrolled through and saw he'd been liking everyone's photos but hers. It was hard to ignore the way his hearts were speckled across other accounts, boosting their presence and lessening hers. Hearts were important. Hearts kept her in business. Hearts weren't just likes — they were what kept her alive.

Tom insisted, though, that they weren't a big deal. Their disagreement on the matter began to cool things between them, though they were all smiles when they posted pictures online. Hailey wondered if he stayed with her to keep his gained popularity online, attaching himself to her influence. If that were the case, the least he could do was keep her afloat by liking just one of her damn posts.

"Jesus Christ, Hailey, will you lay off of me?" It was their third fight in two weeks. Hailey had posted several photos ahead of her weekly Instagram Live, and Tom hadn't liked a single one, not even the one where Hailey wrote *I love you, Tom* while making a heart with her fingers. "It's not that important!" he said.

"It is!" Hailey cried. "It's a video I want people to see, where we'll tell everyone we're moving in together for our six-month anniversary! How's it going to look when you're not even liking my pictures?"

"It's going to look like we're filming a video together! You know a thousand people are gonna watch it anyway —"

"And we should get a thousand more, but I get drop-offs when people stop liking my posts." Hailey wasn't exaggerating. She'd only gotten two offers from companies that week to promote their wares, and a photo of her breakfast that morning — an açaí bowl with homemade keto granola — had gotten a hundred fewer likes than a similar photo the week before. Hailey worried that she'd only continue to fall.

Tom, though, wasn't worried at all — which bothered Hailey more than any lack of likes. "It doesn't matter," he said.

"It does! How does it look when my boyfriend doesn't like my posts, when he goes around liking everyone else's pictures and not mine?"

"No one cares!"

"Everyone cares!" Hailey sped towards Tom and grabbed his phone before he could react. "Everyone watches us, and everyone can see when you don't like my stuff."

"Give me my phone!" Tom wrestled with Hailey for the phone before she could get to her page from his account, where she planned to mass-like every post from the past week.

"They're not just hearts!" she continued. Hailey spun and yanked away from Tom, which caused him to stumble back. He began to fall, and Hailey sent him down faster by hitting him in the chest with his phone. "They're likes —"

Tom's head struck the coffee table. The glass top cracked but didn't shatter. Hailey yanked him up by his shoulders.

"And when you don't like my posts —" Hailey slammed his face against the iron corner of the table — "you bury me!"

Hailey slammed Tom's head against the table one last time, then threw his limp body against the wall. Blood smeared from his face onto the wall as he slid lifeless onto the floor.

Hailey stood still and waited for Tom to move. When he didn't, she walked to his body and placed her fingers against his neck. His heart didn't beat.

Hailey knew this was bad.

She also knew she was supposed to be live in ninety minutes.

She'd find a better way to deal with Tom later. For now, she rolled him into her bedroom and shoved him under the bed, careful to bend in his feet so his shoes wouldn't be visible. She cleaned the trail of blood leading to her room, then scrubbed the table and placed a colorful cloth mat over the crack in the glass. The wall would have to wait until she could buy paint. Wiping the blood would just make the stain worse.

Once she was done, she sat on the couch and tried to collect her bearings. Tom was dead. People would wonder where he was. People would ask about him. She wondered what she'd say when they noticed that Tom was no longer in her feed. Hailey wondered if she should begin scrubbing Tom from her profile now. She had relationship statuses to change, his accounts to unfollow.

But doing that now would only prompt more questions. Why had they disconnected? Did they break up? Where was Tom?

Hailey brought herself out of her thoughts, shook her head, and looked at her phone. She would have to buy time — and the best way was to act normal. She picked up her phone. She'd do her live episode without him. She had before. And before that, she'd post a selfie.

"Hi everyone!" Hailey waved into the camera of her phone. Her laptop sat open beside her so she could monitor comments and likes on her feed while she recorded her Instagram Live on her phone. It was a lot of windows and a lot of people to watch, but Hailey was used to it. She smiled as she greeted her faceless followers. She couldn't see who she was waving to, but hearts began to swim around her face as her viewers liked that she was there.

"It's Thursday night," she continued. "And that means it's time to check in with you before my awesome weekend! As always, you can send me questions, and I'll answer them while I talk about what's been going on lately. So, yesterday I went to a really great sandwich shop in Dupont Circle, and —"

A question interrupted Hailey almost immediately. They always did, but while Hailey expected the question, it still caught her off-guard: *Where's Tom?*

Hailey smiled and looked back at her camera. "Someone's already asked me about Tom! He's not here tonight. He's out and about, but hopefully he'll be back for next week's video." She made a mental note to set the virtual stage for a dramatic exit on Tom's behalf, where, after months of love and joy and visiting the hottest places together, he'd straight-up ghost her. That was why he wasn't online through his various accounts: he was avoiding her. Maybe she'd get everyone to search for him. She tried not to chuckle at the thought of all of her followers going on a wild-goose chase for someone who was dead — nor frown at the thought of all of them flocking away from her feed in search of his.

A swarm of typed sighs and sad-face emojis came through, and Hailey sighed as she slumped her shoulders for effect. "I know, you guys, I miss him, too. But we'll see him and his beautiful face again soon."

Hailey heard a ding, which signaled that someone liked one of her previous posts. She looked at her laptop and checked which post it was as she continued to speak. "Anyway, this sandwich shop, Bahn Mots, is a Vietnamese fusion place which offers new takes on the classic —"

Hailey stopped as she checked her notifications. Her breakfast that morning, the one with fewer likes than the breakfast she'd posted before, had one new like — from TommyBoy89.

Hailey blinked, then refreshed the photo. She didn't see Tom's username, just the thousands of likes that had been there before.

Hailey ignored it. It was probably a mistake.

"Sorry guys," she said with a shrug. "I got distracted by someone liking my breakfast this morning. Did you all try that keto granola? I couldn't believe how good it was, especially since it didn't have any oats."

A flock of hearts flew through her screen. One follower wrote, *It looked so good! I'm making it tomorrow!* Another added, *I bet keto's why your face is so pretty.*

"Aw, thanks to the follower who said my face is pretty. It's just average, guys —" Hailey patted her cheeks as she looked from side to side — "and I keep it decent-looking with good food, good health, and this awesome oat scrub I just started using. It —"

Before Hailey could talk about the soap she'd promised the organic start-up she'd promote in exchange for free products and a boost on their channels, she got another like on an old post. It was a selfie she'd posted the day before to show off her new makeup, a blue eye shadow that Tom said made her eyes look like an autumn sky over her freckles. Hailey shared his comment in her post and tagged him, yet still, it had gone unliked.

Until now. TommyBoy89 liked the post.

"What the hell?" Hailey muttered. She didn't realize she'd spoken out loud until a series of questions came through from her followers, all various forms of *What?*

"Oh, nothing," Hailey replied with a smile, though it was weaker than it'd been before. "I just got distracted by another like on my makeup selfie from yesterday."

Another question came through, and Hailey readied a response on who the company was, or which colors would best suit which skin tones. The question, though, wasn't about her eye shadow. *Hey, sorry I'm late. Where's Tom?*

Hailey kept her smile but sighed through it. She hoped it was quiet enough to not get picked up on the mic. "I just got another question about Tom," she said. She knew avoiding questions about him would cause more suspicion than ignoring them. "You all must really miss him!"

Another cluster of hearts swam across the screen, and Hailey tried not to glower at Tom's popularity. She and Tom were popular. That was what the hearts were for: the two of them.

"Like I said before, I don't know where he is tonight," Hailey said with as much enthusiasm as she could muster. "But hopefully we'll see him soon."

Hailey heard another ding. She closed her eyes at the sound. All she'd wanted when Tom was alive was just one heart, one like to show her he was watching her online. Now that he was dead, his hearts were all she heard — and they were the last thing she wanted.

The sound of a question made her open her eyes. She read: *What's wrong?*

Hailey smiled again. She had to remember she was live. "Nothing, sorry," she said. "I'm getting a lot of likes again. Now, this scrub."

Another ding. Another like. Hailey ignored it. She picked up the scrub and continued, "It's from a new company called Oatshine, and —"

Ding.

"They use all-organic oats and fruits —"

Ding. Ding.

"Which sounds like breakfast, and really, it is like breakfast, but for your —"

Dingdingdingdingdingdingding —

"WHAT?" Hailey slammed down the scrub and checked her notifications. She saw several likes, all of them for pictures she'd posted over the past six months — and all of them from TommyBoy89.

It couldn't be. Tom was dead beneath her bed, and his phone lay still on the coffee table next to her. Hailey checked each notification to see if he was indeed liking her pictures, but when she refreshed them, Tom's likes would disappear amongst the thousands of others, part of a number that Hailey lost count of within minutes of her pictures going viral.

But as he had in life, Tom stood out from the rest. His username clamored for her attention as she tried to keep up with his hearts. The likes became a steady beat that Hailey knew she'd have to ignore. "It's a soap I've started using every day, and if you use the code HailStorm20, you'll get twenty percent off your first order."

The dings ceased. Hailey sighed with relief. "Now, this weekend," she continued. "I've got a lot of fun stuff planned —
"

A follower asked her a question: *Didn't you have some big announcement with Tom?*

Hailey's grin stayed frozen in place as she replied, "Some of you remember that Tom and I were going to have a big announcement tonight." How could they forget? She'd talked about it for a week to get their followers excited. She'd talked about it, but Tom had not. Tom had posted pictures of his dinner, a couple selfies with her, and only one picture of her the night before, with a caption saying he'd have something special to share about a special someone very soon. It'd gotten lots of likes. So had Hailey's announcements — but not one like from him. Hailey seethed a little as she continued, "But, as I've mentioned a couple times now, he's not here; and I don't want to say anything without him."

Another ding, a single one this time. Hailey forgot her followers as she opened the picture that was liked. It was a close-up she'd taken of Tom after one month of dating, one that emphasized his eyes. The same beautiful eyes she'd seen when she clicked through to his profile all those months ago. Hailey bit her lip and tried not to hyperventilate despite her heartbeat climbing in time with her notifications. The thrum of dings thrashed in her ears as she stared at him staring at her.

One of her viewers asked, *What's wrong?*

"N-nothing," Hailey replied, though she couldn't smile.

You look awful, another follower wrote.

Eat more açaí bowls, a third one quipped.

A swarm of hearts flooded the screen. Hailey knew they weren't for her, but for the viewer's joke. She furrowed her brow and said as calmly as she could, "Really, I'm okay."

Ding. Ding. Ding.

"I'm just ready for the weekend, and —"

Ready for Tom to come back?

Hailey paused, then said, "Yes." She took a breath as she composed herself. A little vulnerability would only make her story about being ghosted all the more tragic. "Yes, I'm more than ready to see him again. I miss him, even though it's only been a short while since I've —"

A ding snapped in her ears, and she looked at her laptop before she could stop herself. She clicked through when she saw that the notification wasn't just a like, but a comment. Hailey saw the first picture they'd taken together, one she'd snapped the afternoon after their first date. Tom kissed her cheek, and she grinned at the camera. Underneath the picture, TommyBoy89 had written, *Hi.*

Hailey covered her mouth and tried not to scream. The dings became a steady stream once more — *dingdingdingdingdingdingding* — and she moved her hands to her ears to quiet their call. A question popped up on her screen and glared her in the eye: *Yeah, where's Tom?*

Their questions had to stop. Tom's likes had to stop. Tom had to be stopped. She'd stopped him before, and everyone would see it and know that they should stop, too, before she lost her mind.

"You want to know where Tom is?" Hailey snapped.

She jumped up and stormed into her bedroom. Hailey dragged his body from beneath the bed and wrapped her arm around his shoulder to steady him as she held up her phone. "Here he is! Here's Tom! So stop asking me, stop asking where he is, and for God's sake —" she stared into his open, lifeless eyes and his bloodied, broken face — "STOP LIKING MY PICS!"

STICK FIGURE FAMILY

Chelsea hurried through the parking lot at Trader Joe's. It was always crazy on Saturdays, and she usually tried to avoid the hubbub of suburban parents and their cranky kids. She'd run out of her favorite soap that morning, though, and would need more before the weekend was over.

The parking lot was a quagmire of vans, shopping carts, and people. A couple bickered over something trivial as they walked by her. A child screamed in her cart as her father tried to sweet-talk her into behaving.

Chelsea closed her eyes as she tried to keep her composure.

"Watch out!" a woman's voice called.

Chelsea looked toward the voice, then felt sharp plastic whack against her legs. She cursed, and a woman in a blue knitted poncho pulled back the cart that had hit her.

"I'm sorry," the woman said. "I was lost in my own world and didn't even see you."

Chelsea glared at her and rubbed her aching knees.

The woman had straight brown hair, as dull and faded as her grey leggings. She pressed a button and unlocked the minivan next to them. Chelsea saw a line of stick figures on the window. She tried not to roll her eyes. Stick figure families were so sickeningly charming. *No one cares how many smiling kids you have*, she thought.

"Do you need something?" the woman asked. She had the slightest hint of irritation in her voice. She had some nerve, being the one who hit Chelsea in the first place.

"No," Chelsea said. She walked off without a word. All she needed was to get out of the parking lot.

Camila checked her hair in the mirror before pulling out of the parking lot at Trader Joe's. She hadn't even seen that girl with the messy blonde bun and the deep-set frown. She wondered what was wrong with her. Hitting her with the cart had been an accident — an honest mistake. Camila sighed as she pulled out of the lot and turned on the radio. The girl wasn't her concern.

She drove down the road. The strip malls and condos disappeared behind her as she made her way towards her favorite spot: the lake behind her parents' old cabin. It was her favorite spot to be alone and catch her breath after a busy morning chasing after the kids.

Camila parked her van and took in the sparkling lake in front of her. The surface lay still, with no one around to drop rocks in its waters or cast lines in search of fish.

She smiled as she opened the trunk. She had a box of crackers and a block of her favorite cheese waiting for her.

Camila set the grocery bag on the ground, then lifted the limp bodies of two children from the floor of the trunk. They'd been running through the woods near her apartment, and they should've known better than to wake her up with their shouts.

Once they were in the lake — and once she'd washed her hands — Camila ate her snack and stared out over the water. The surface bubbled a little as the bodies sank, but it soon stood as still as it had before.

Camila got to her feet and brushed stray blades of grass from her leggings. She approached her van, then dug through her purse. Before she got in, she stuck two new stick figures on her van's back window.

CRANBERRY

Christy's favorite holiday was Thanksgiving. She loved the fancy tablecloth her mother set out, and loved watching her father carve the turkey. Christy wasn't allowed to help — at eight years old, she was still too young to handle a knife — but her father let her watch so she would know how to do it when she was older. He slipped her a piece of skin, and she loved the way it cracked in her mouth and coated her tongue with salt and grease.

She ate her piece of turkey skin with a smile as her mother opened a can of cranberry sauce and poured it in a bowl. The sauce came out as a cylinder and kept its form, with the ridges of the can rippling down the sides.

Christy and her parents laughed at the sight of it. "It kind of looks like you," her father said as he pinched a roll of fat on Christy's waist.

Christy lost her smile. Her mother chuckled softly as she cut the cranberry sauce with a butter knife. It fell to pieces in the bowl, which her mother topped with walnuts.

"Going to enjoy that sauce, Cranberry?" her dad said, smiling and pinching her fat one more time. He returned to carving the turkey. Christy swallowed the skin and felt it scratch her throat on the way down.

Christy had always known she was more plump than normal. The kids at school called her fat before whatever insult they wanted to throw her way. Fat nerd. Fat idiot. Fat girl. Fat was what they saw first. Christy had learned to absorb their insults and turn them into white noise.

It was harder, though, to ignore her parents. Christy noticed as they watched her plate and took note of how much food disappeared, and how quickly. She could almost hear them counting the pounds she added to her waist, pounds that formed rings which showed her to the world the way the rings of a trunk showed the age of a tree.

As Christy grew, she tried to stop her rings from growing with her. Her breasts grew out, but so did her stomach. The hair on her belly and legs was only made worse by the fat it covered. The monthly bleeding made her feel less bloated, but not less fat. She tried to eat well, tried to eat her fruits and vegetables and keep the candy down to treats at Halloween and Christmas. It was never enough.

On the day before the start of ninth grade, and after a back-to-school shopping session where her mother had clucked about shopping for larger sizes, Christy stood naked and alone in her room. She pushed the fat until her skin was against her bones. She sighed as she looked at her newfound waist, set in perfect symmetry with her hips and her breasts. She pulled the fat beneath her chin and tucked it under her thumbs. Her jawbone peeked at her, her skin stretched against her skull. She kneaded her arms and legs, the bones pressing against her muscles and showing her what they could offer. Approval. Appeal. Affection. She wished her bones would slice through the fat and take their rightful place against her skin.

Wishing, though, wasn't enough. Christy had to make it happen herself — and she had to try harder than she'd ever tried before.

Christy took extra care as high school progressed and

her body grew into itself. She imagined her parents watching her every bite even when she was at school. She chose the healthiest foods, took longer walks, tried to do crunches in her room. Nothing worked — until, suddenly, it did.

All of a sudden, Christy's efforts clicked into place. Her diet smoothies, scant peanut-butter sandwiches, and long walks began to pay off. Her clothes got bigger, and she grew smaller. She lost weight — noticeable weight — and it stayed off. She graduated from high school with the body she'd longed for ever since she was a little girl and first felt her folds spill over her jeans.

"Have fun," her mother said as they finished moving Christy into her college dorm.

"Watch out for the dining hall," her father joked as he patted her waist.

Her mother chuckled. "The freshman fifteen is always a killer." She winked at Christy.

Christy waited until they were gone before she allowed her smile to disappear. She ran her hands over her waist, her chest, her chin and her shoulders. She felt the bones beneath and felt comforted by how they pressed against her skin. As long as she could feel the bones, she'd be okay.

Christy made sure throughout her first semester that the feel of her bones never left her palms. She monitored her plate at the dining hall. She was extra careful with dessert. If she allowed herself an indulgence, like a cookie or a brownie, she thought of her former self with every bite to remind herself to not gain weight and lose her bones. Dessert became so stressful that she almost avoided it altogether. Eating was a game of chance — one that Christy was determined not to lose.

Christy avoided gaining weight, and did one better by losing more. She felt her tapered waist and the ceiling of her ribs. She'd lie down and feel her hip bones jut out over her waistband. As long as she could feel her bones, she knew she was safe.

Christy came home for Thanksgiving feeling proud. She didn't even mind the sight of the rippled mold of cranberry sauce falling into the bowl, its rolls of jellied fat quivering into place. Her father chuckled as her mother grabbed a butter knife.

"The sauce has its ribs sticking out," he said as he pinched Christy's bones. "Kind of like you, Cranberry."

The nickname struck Christy in the heart. She could feel her heart ramming against her ribs. The ribs and bones that added to her body, that stuck out, that made it so large that it was always in the way.

The scraping of metal against ceramic rang in Christy's ears. Christy watched her mother slice the cranberry sauce into manageable pieces, watched her father carve the turkey and set the salted skin in pieces on the plate. That was the only way she could be perfect. It was the only way that any of them could be perfect.

Her mind, her heart, and her bones clanged and scraped inside of her so loudly she could barely hear her father shout when she wrested the knife from his grasp. She could hardly feel her mother's hands pull at her wrist as she took the blade to her waist.

They all would be in pieces soon. Soon, they all would be perfect.

QUADRAPOCALYPSE

The train lurched as the Metro moved towards Foggy Bottom. It was moving through the tunnel Morgan always wished they'd leave the fastest, the one connecting Virginia to DC, beneath the Potomac River. She tried to avoid thinking about how she spent a portion of each day underwater just to get to work. Those thoughts inevitably led to wondering about just how strong the tunnel walls were against the river's current.

Like her fellow commuters, though, she managed to distract herself from such thoughts and make it into the District each day. Some people read the paper, others listened to music. Morgan read a book. Her commute was the best time to read.

Lurch. "Train moving," the conductor said.

Stop. "Train holding. We thank you for your patience."

She'd heard that refrain at least four times. Morgan sighed as she put away her book. She couldn't read with the train pitching her body back and forth.

Morgan's eyes wandered across her fellow passengers. Most of them stared into nothingness as they waited to get to work. One passenger, a woman in a yolk-yellow raincoat, looked into nothingness for a long time. She seemed lost in thought, so lost in thought that she was the only one who didn't notice when she dropped her phone.

It landed with a thud that snapped the commuters from their distractions. A chorus of variations on "Ma'am, you dropped your phone" and "Is it broken?" rang through the train. The woman waved in thanks as she picked it up. The screen had cracked, and Morgan saw its jagged smile, a kaleidoscope of broken light and pixels on its shattered face. Morgan thought she saw four shadows fly past people's feet. She blinked, as did the lights on the train.

The lights came back on. Morgan shook her head, and figured the shadows were just from the lights.

Morgan noticed that the train was still holding. It hadn't moved an inch.

"We'll be holding here momentarily. Thank you for your patience."

The commuters sighed and rolled their eyes. A group of tourists stared at the Metro map as they hoped to find their way around the city. Morgan studied the map to give herself something to do, even though she knew the city well already. The map was a colorful spider whose legs wrapped around the District's four corners: Northwest, Northeast, Southeast, and Southwest. The Metro's lines extended to all of the city's quadrants. Morgan wondered where everyone would go once they were released.

Southeast

Danica cursed as she skidded across the slick granite sidewalk in her heels. She walked as fast as she could through the drizzle. She had a lunch meeting at Tortilla Coast, and she was already late. The damp sidewalks didn't help, but the slow-moving congressional aides and tourists visiting Capitol Hill were what really slowed her down.

Why are there still so many people out in this rain? she thought with a frown as she maneuvered around fellow pedestrians and tried not to poke them with her umbrella. It'd been raining off and on almost all week. At least today, it was just a persistent drizzle and not a downpour.

Danica heard a gurgling sound below her. She looked down, then saw burst of water spit up through the manhole ahead of her and onto the road.

A group of staffers cursed as the cuffs of their pants were dampened. Danica shook her head. Even though today's rain was just a drizzle, one had to expect residual flooding from the Potomac to find its way onto the city's streets.

More water spewed from the manhole. Danica saw that manholes down the sidewalk did the same. She looked back at the one closest to her, transfixed, along with several others.

The next sputter brought a wave of putrid water and what looked like paws and feet within its current. Danica covered her mouth as the water trickled away and the paws, feet, and fur hobbled into a standing position.

"A rat!" a man next to her cried. Several rats peered at their newfound place above ground. They were so laden with water that their bellies protruded and rippled as they moved along the street. Despite their weight, they moved quickly towards the people staring at them.

A blonde woman acted quickly — she stabbed a rat with her umbrella before it could crawl over her shoes. It popped like a balloon, water mixed with blood and guts flying onto her dress.

She held up her umbrella in triumph, but the victory was short-lived. The water didn't run off of her legs, but rather up her body. She seemed to dissolve under its current. Her clothes blackened into mildew and her screams became garbled as mud spewed from her throat.

The others weren't much better off. The rats crawled over their bodies, their fur leaving slicked trails across their skin that turned people's bodies to algae and mold. They became green and oily remnants of flesh, ones that washed away beneath the drizzle.

Danica turned and ran before the rats could reach her. The sidewalk beneath her grew softer with every step. The rats and water spewing from the manholes seemed to be turning the sidewalk into a muddied shore, one that would soon be as thick and damp as an ocean floor.

Danica's sprint ended as the heel of her shoe dug into the sidewalk. She twisted it off and ran further, hoping that the increasing slickness on her foot was only from the rain on the sidewalk.

Southwest

Andre tied his apron as he prepared to open the crab shack. He was alone, as he was every morning. He liked to arrive before anyone else so that his food would be ready all the quicker. His fellow restaurant owners were his neighbors and friends, but they were also his competition.

He'd worked on the wharf for almost twenty years, long before the wharf officially became "the Wharf," with strings of lights along the dock that led potential customers to concert halls, distilleries, and expensive restaurants.

Still, people came to his shack each day wanting a steaming plate of crabs covered in Old Bay to eat by the water. Andre just hoped they could reach him. The rain all week had flooded the docks, and only a raised wooden bridge allowed hungry customers passage.

A loud pop distracted Andre from preparing his pans. He looked toward the new restaurants on the Wharf. One of the lights on the string along the dock had exploded. It set off an identical pop. Each bulb burst, one by one. Sparks flew up as the shards of glass flew out.

Andre moved to the counter so he could see. The sparks weren't small by any means. They looked like orange snakes that spiraled and coiled around the buildings. As they wrapped around the structures, each burst into flames. They crackled and hissed as the dock connecting them became a river of flame flowing into the water.

Andre pulled out his cellphone, ready to call the fire department. Before he could, the sound of an explosion burst to his left. The streetlamps began to explode. Snakes and sparks did not come forth. These creatures of fire were much bigger. They flew from the glass, wings of red and blue crackling against the sky as they soared further east. They ran their hands along the sidewalk and grass like people letting their fingers loll in the water during a boat ride. Everything they touched turned to fire. It was a flame without smoke and burned without turning things to ash.

Andre looked at the wooden platform leading to his crab shack, then the water surrounding it on all sides. He'd never been so grateful for a flood before.

A flicker of light caught his attention. He looked beyond the platform. The pyre that had been the Wharf did not extinguish when it touched the water. It continued to burn, using the river as oil for its flame.

Andre looked back down. He saw tiny snakes of gold swimming through the flooded waters toward his restaurant, like minnows rushing towards a morning snack.

Northeast

Portia just wanted to get to class, but the bustle of H Street made that nearly impossible. She'd been promised that the budding H Street Corridor would be the perfect place for a college student to study and party in the District. The marketing downplayed how long it would take to get from H Street to Howard University, and how often she'd be waiting for a bus if she wanted to party anywhere but H Street's overpriced clubs and hipster restaurants.

She walked with a frown as she adjusted her backpack. A truck drove by and belched a cloud of smoke. Portia waved the smoke from her face and tried not to breathe it in, though she could feel it settle in her nostrils. She made a mental note to use her neti pot that night.

A breeze blew the smoke away faster than her hand could hope to accomplish. Portia smiled and thanked God for a bit of wind to help her on her commute.

"Ow!"

Portia looked towards the cry and saw a man on the sidewalk in front of her. He stood up and brushed gravel from his knees. He saw Portia looking at him. Before she could turn away, he smiled and shrugged. "Guess the wind caught me off-guard," he said with a laugh.

Portia gave a small smile back. He was cute — even though he sported an unfortunate man bun — and had a nice laugh.

Both were distracted from the other by two more screams to their left. They turned and saw a family of three sprawled on the sidewalk. The child, who looked no older than five, began to cry. His parents lay stunned on the ground.

"Are you okay?" Portia called as she rushed towards them. A gust of wind stopped her. It froze her in her tracks, then knocked her to the ground. "Ow!" she screamed as she rubbed her aching butt.

"Let me help —" the cute man began to say, but he was pushed back down before he could make it to her. He seemed to be pulled back by an invisible hook. Portia skidded across the sidewalk. Though the wind whipped through her clothes, she swore she felt a multitude of fingers grip her body and pull her back.

People all around skidded and fell on the sidewalk, as if they were being bandied about by small, invisible hands. Portia didn't know what to make of the wind. It was drizzly today, but not stormy; and hurricane season was still weeks away.

The wind grew stronger. More people fell, and with greater force. Heads began to crack and bleed on the sidewalk. Skinned knees turned into scraped bodies. Portia watched in horror as the cute man was lifted by a gust of wind and thrown through the glass of the Irish pub she'd just had dinner in the night before.

She screamed as she was lifted off the ground, then dropped with a thud on the curb. Another truck rolled by, and she thanked God that she'd fallen on the curb and not on the street. She grabbed onto a streetlamp to try and stay steady.

The truck came to a stop, held back and knocked about by the wind. Before it fell, it belched out one last cloud of smoke.

Portia didn't register the truck blowing over, nor the screams of the people crushed beneath it. All she saw was the large, outstretched hand the truck's exhaust made visible. Just before the wind blew the smoke into nothing, she saw clawed fingers stretch and zoom towards her, ready to bat her away.

Northwest

Gita's favorite thing about her apartment was the view of the zoo. It was surrounded by lush trees and shoots of bamboo. She could see the tops of the trees from her top-floor apartment, and she liked to imagine all of the animals living there beneath the canopy.

She stirred milk into her morning tea and checked her phone while she sipped. An alert from the *Woodley Park Buzz*, their neighborhood e-newsletter, blinked up at her:

Zookeepers ask neighborhood to be on alert for a missing flamingo from the zoo. Do not approach. Email bird's location to —

Gita didn't read the rest. She remembered when a red panda had gone missing for almost two days. Someone found it in their backyard. Someone would likely find the flamingo resting in their koi pond, or dipping its beak into one of the puddles left over from the flash flooding in Rock Creek Park.

Gita set down her tea and looked back outside. The rain had left the trees and bamboo looking even more lush than before. They almost seemed to be sitting outside of her balcony.

Another alert beeped from her phone. Gita read another note from the *Woodley Park Buzz*:

Zookeepers ask neighborhood to be on alert for a missing orangutan from the zoo. Do not approach. Email orangutan's —

Gita furrowed her brow as she set down her phone. An orangutan had never escaped from the zoo before. She figured, though, that an orangutan would be easy to spot once Woodley Park was on the lookout for it. There were trees, but not many. People would notice an orangutan on the loose.

She looked back outside. Her eyes widened. The view looked more like a forest than it had before. The trees blotted out the sky and seemed to surround her building on all sides. It had to be an illusion, her eyes playing tricks on her as she took in all the green that had come from the week's rain.

Horns began to blare from the street below. Gita rolled her eyes, then walked towards the living room window, which looked out over the street. It was her least favorite view, as it reminded her that she was very much in a city. Normally she'd ignore it, but a part of her wondered if the orangutan was in the street.

Gita looked out and almost dropped her phone. Vines as thick as rope shot into the street from all sides. They carved through buildings and cracked the pavement. A menagerie of zoo animals ran over their newfound bridge to freedom.

The human residents of Woodley Park weren't so lucky. Cars and people were coiled in the foliage and slammed against buildings. One shop owner tried to take a knife to a vine coming for his window. The vine wrapped around his leg, and two leaves grabbed his knife. Gita looked away just as the leaf placed the blade against the shop owner's throat.

Gita's phone beeped once more. She looked down and read yet another note from the *Woodley Park Buzz*:

Zookeepers ask neighborhood to be on alert for a missing tiger from the zoo. Do not —

A loud crash interrupted her. Gita turned, wondering with mounting fear if she'd see the tiger standing in her kitchen. Like the animals that climbed from the zoo to the street, it could have used the trees and bamboo outside her window as a ladder.

The trees and bamboo she loved to look out over each morning crashed through her table and spilled her tea. The branches and vines moved towards her as quickly as centipedes moving through dirt. They wrapped around her ankles, and Gita cried out as their flesh stung her skin. The vines yanked her onto the floor and dragged her towards her overgrown balcony. Her phone beeped one last time as it flew from her hands.

Metro

"We're continuing to hold. Thank you for your patience."

Morgan had lost track of how long they'd been holding. She'd already finished her book and had grown tired of looking at the same frustrated passengers over and over again. No one could get any signal in the tunnel. No one knew when they would be moving — not even the train conductor, who simply assured them they'd be moving momentarily.

A loud crash broke everyone from their frustrated trance. Morgan looked out the window, but didn't see anything.

The crash sounded again. The car in front of them knocked against the tunnel's walls, as if punched by the wind. Morgan wondered how wind could get underground.

The crash was replaced by a pop. A blaze of fire shot past the train. It almost appeared to have wings. There was a thud on top of the car. The ceiling dissolved like ice cream on a sidewalk, and flaming claws seeped through the metal.

As frightened passengers fled, a vine crashed through the emergency exit. It coiled around the metal poles and broke through the seats. Passengers tried to move to the next car, but the wind that knocked the car in front of them punched passengers into the waiting hands of the flames and the plants.

Morgan hid under her seat and looked for an opening. She thought she saw the woman in the yolk-yellow raincoat slip away with a smile as a family of tourists ran from the vines. She looked at the walls of the tunnel and wished that the river she feared so much would wash away the fire and foliage.

Morgan heard water, but not from the walls.

A putrid stream trickled into the train, dissolving the carpet and turning the seats into mildew. She watched as the elements did away with them all.

Morgan heard one last call over everyone's screams: "We'll be holding here momentarily. Thank you for your patience."

SOMEONE TO SHARE MY NIGHTMARES

Kristin's favorite director was in town. He'd been there for almost a month, buried in a grassy knoll at the top of the local cemetery. His stone was the largest, a beacon whose notebooks, flowers, statues, and other items left in tribute cast a gilded shadow on the graves that were unknown to all except their families and friends left behind.

Jonathan Ransom had not been born in Kristin's town. He hadn't even lived there. But he made sure he'd stay there in death, buried in Thornhill Cemetery in the small town of Creekwood, North Carolina.

Ransom's films were haunting portraits of the South, bringing forth that unsettled quiet that most Southerners only knew as a feeling or a sense of innate displeasure with one's surroundings—a quiet anger they couldn't quite place. Ransom manifested that anger into ghosts, shadows, and monsters. He formed them into shapes, created characters that explained Kristin's deepest suspicions about where she lived. His work was celebrated across the country, and his last three films had each garnered more praise than the next.

Ransom claimed that in Creekwood, he'd found his muse. Its empty trees, barren even in summer, and blackened creeks that flowed inches deep brought a mood to his films that actors never could. Kristin knew those scenes well, had known them ever since she first entered the woods that Ransom found delightful. She always tried to see him shoot. He was famous for only shooting at dusk or at dawn, and in the quietest corners of Creekwood that even the locals managed to avoid.

If she'd had the chance to meet him, she would've been able to tell him to avoid those corners.

Ransom's death was called an accident. A local found him at the bottom of a ditch, and his head was bent in an unnatural angle against the stone. Ransom's camera lay shattered next to him, all the film exposed and ruined. No one would see what Ransom saw ever again.

Kristin always knew there was something wrong with the woods outside of her house. Its trees bent at odd shapes, and they never seemed to bear blossoms or fruit. Yet they lived, year in and year out. Birds built nests in their crevices, squirrels burrowed in their holes. Eggs fell to the ground before they hatched, and hawks left the bloodied remains of the squirrels on the roots.

The forest's horrors began to appear in her dreams as early as elementary school. Kristin would fall asleep and, in her mind, she'd wander into a forest that no longer hid behind the trappings of flora and fauna. Between craggy trees stood corpses, their mouths frozen into a scream as their arms and hands stretched to the sky alongside the branches. The leaves on the forest floor were strewn with hair and teeth. Each nightmare ended with smoke curling at Kristin's feet and the glow of two eyes blinking in front of her. When she awoke in the safety of her room, she'd vow to stay away from such a dangerous place.

And yet, Kristin couldn't stay away. She'd walk by the woods and feel as if the smoke in her dreams were nipping at her ankles like a wolf puppy, welcoming her into its wild domain. And when she entered the woods, she felt an eerie sense of calm, like whatever had beckoned her was grateful for the company. She knew when she was welcome, and when she should leave. It was as if the demon the eyes in her nightmares belonged to allowed her in so long as she listened to their whispers and left when they told her.

All of his fans mourned his passing, but Kristin also mourned the loss of someone else—perhaps the only someone—who understood those woods the way she had. When Jonathan Ransom spoke of the forests of Creekwood, it had been like listening to her own thoughts made clear. Whenever she'd shared them with anyone, they called her ridiculous or, at best, said she had the potential to write horror. Jonathan Ransom wrote horror, but what made his horror so compelling was his belief in it being real. Not a belief in monsters or ghosts, but a belief in something sinister, something made manifest in the limited ways people could see it. Kristin saw it in her nightmares. Ransom gave her nightmares life.

Kristin knew deep down that the woods were the woods. She wouldn't give in to the seductive pull of the nightmare of the forest until she told herself emphatically that it was a nightmare, a fantasy she enjoyed the same as any horror film. It was her imagination—one that, until Jonathan Ransom took up residence beneath the grassy knoll at the end of Thornhill Cemetery, she thought she'd shared with someone else.

But Kristin wasn't going to the cemetery today. She was going straight to the source of her current pain: the ditch that had taken Jonathan Ransom's life. She walked through the silent woods, quiet even though it was still the afternoon. She carried a rose to leave at the ditch.

As she neared the site of Ransom's death, the silence slowly began to slip away. She thought she heard a rustling, but as she got closer, it became a trickle. There were no creeks in the forest, at least not close to here.

Kristin entered the clearing where the ditch had once been. In its place was a rushing creek. The stone that broke Jonathan Ransom's neck was now covered by rushing water.

Kristin sighed. The rainstorms from the previous week must have left their remnants in the woods. Or else the woods wanted to wash him away from her memory for good.

She tossed the rose in the water, then walked away. She'd had enough of the forest for one afternoon.

"I see demons every day. I want others to see them too."

Jonathan Ransom's eyes pierced through the lens as he spoke. His voice trembled from Kristin's phone and settled in her ears as she sat in her car. He spoke calmly of the things that scared most everyone else.

"I want others to see what I see," he continued as he spoke with Chelsea Davenport in a rare interview. It was three years old, between his first Oscar and his last completed film. "And I don't want them to deny that they saw it. That's why I lay demons bare in imagery that exists without special effects. Tree branches, shadows, a dark creek. All contain demons, and film helps me show those demons in ways that others can't avoid."

"So, you believe in demons?" Chelsea asked off-camera. The camera wouldn't dare leave Ransom's face. He was so stoic, so calm about fear. The camera wanted to confront viewers with Ransom's calmness. It was more unsettling than any demon he spoke of.

"Yes," he replied, as if Chelsea had asked if the sky

were blue or if chocolate was delicious. "But not in the way you're thinking."

"What way am I thinking?"

"The way everyone does: silly monsters summoned from Hell. Candles, the wrong incantation, fire. Horns and cloven feet. Blood and fangs, tits and cocks in wretched proportions." His smile grew. "Did I embarrass you, Ms. Davenport?"

"We don't really talk about tits and cocks on network TV."

"Then you shouldn't be speaking to me about monsters." He chuckled, then continued, "But I don't believe in those demons. Those are the demons everyone believes in, the ones they make up so they can pretend that evil isn't human. That it isn't a part of the world, a chaos as inherent to living as oxygen. It's all a part of life. Evil, like goodness, is very much human; and all we can do when we see it is try to stop it."

"Or in your case, film it."

"I film it in an effort to stop it. I was drawn to film because film magnifies life in ways that help us see what we miss every day. I wanted to magnify the demons so that people would see them more easily."

"You seem to be frightening them, if reviews of your last film are any indication."

Ransom smiled. It cast a pleasant chill on Kristin's heart, like a breeze breaking through the August humidity.

"Isn't fear what compels us all?" Ransom asked.

The YouTube clip stopped, and part two of the interview was about to begin. Kristin stopped the video and put her phone away, then looked out across the field toward the woods.

Water running over where Ransom had died had

bothered her more than it should. It almost seemed like the woods delighted in Ransom's death and had seen his flesh as a means of creation. Kristin knew it was silly to think so, and yet she couldn't shake the feeling. Something was wrong with the forest. She'd seen it, and Ransom had seen it too. Had the woods wanted to stop him from seeing it?

She narrowed her eyes at the trees as the late afternoon sun glowed overtop of them. The light was purely August, golden and fat with excess heat. The tree branches stretched toward the sky, begging for rain; and yet they stood proud, knowing that nothing and no one could expose them. Not even a director who'd seen them for what they were.

Kristin saw the woods for what they were. Would the forest do something to her?

She turned off her car and got out. These were crazy thoughts. She needed something to dull those thoughts, and the small bar on the side of the loneliest road in Creekwood would be just the ticket.

Kristin stirred the cherry in her drink. The ice had already begun to melt, rendering her Jack and ginger more watery than a high schooler's eyes when their favorite character died on the CW. Condensation covered the glass and slicked her palms. The only thing more useless than her visit to Jonathan Ransom's death site that day was trying to have a cold drink in a Carolina summer.

"Want me to freshen you up there?"

Kristin looked up and saw Evangeline, the bartender, smiling at her. Kristin managed a weak smile back, then gulped her drink down in three swallows. "Yes please," she said as she set down her glass towards Evangeline's end of the bar.

She grabbed a clean glass and filled it with ice. Jack Daniel's and ginger ale followed, along with another cherry. A line of condensation formed almost as soon as Kristin took the glass.

"You'd never know we fixed the air conditioner last week," Evangeline said.

"You sure it's working?" Doug called from his seat. He was a barfly Kristin was convinced slept in the corner booth.

"Sure, it's working, it's just hot." Regardless, Evangeline waved her hand in front of the lone air conditioning vent over the bar. Kristin sipped her drink and wondered how long it would take to not only forget her wasted afternoon, but the useless conversation happening next to her.

"Excuse me."

Kristin looked up at the unfamiliar voice. Her eyes widened, and she was glad that the man standing in the doorway was facing Evangeline and not her. He was so handsome that Kristin didn't think he could possibly be real. Every feature, from his sandy blond hair to his strong chin, from his dark eyes to his broad shoulders, seemed crafted to elicit lust in anyone who looked at him.

Anyone, maybe, except Evangeline. "Yes?" she asked, with about the same level of interest she'd show any stranger walking into her bar.

"Do you sell food? I've been wandering around all day and I'm starving."

The man was barely sweating. Had he done a glam-up in his car before coming in?

Evangeline smiled and tossed a small bag of potato chips onto the bar. "This is about it," she said. "But you can order delivery here if you want."

"Will do." The man moved towards the bar, and Kristin noticed how close the potato chips were to her seat. She glanced at Evangeline, who winked at her before turning back to the bar to get a refill of Doug's favorite beer.

"This seat taken?" the man asked with a smile as he moved to sit down.

"No. Go ahead." Kristin took a large sip of her drink to try and calm her eyes back into a normal width.

"Thanks." He pulled the chips toward him and immediately became immersed in his phone. Kristin shrugged to herself and turned back to the bar.

"You have any recommendations?" the man asked.

Kristin turned and saw him looking at her. "Recommendations?"

"For food. You live around here?"

"Oh. Yeah, I'm local." Was it that obvious? Her fingers flicked to her hair to straighten it. She stopped herself, then realized her fingers were floating by her cheek. She curled them under her cheek, then her chin. She hoped she didn't look like as much of a spaz as she felt.

The man smiled, and Kristin felt everything in her body calm except for her heart, which beat so hard she could feel it pulse between her thighs. "So, what do you recommend?" he asked.

"Mike's," Kristin replied. "Mike's Deli. They deliver and they make a great turkey club."

"Perfect." The man turned away from her and tapped in his order. Kristin's shoulders fell a little, but when she turned back, she saw a refreshed Jack and ginger in front of her.

"And what'll you have with that club sandwich?" Evangeline asked the man. Kristin kept her eyes away from him.

"I'll have whatever she's having," he answered. Kristin glanced at him and saw him smiling at her. "Seems like she has good taste."

Evangeline gave Kristin a sly look, one Kristin hoped the man didn't notice. "She does," she said as she made the man's drink.

"I have good taste too!" Doug called.

"You like whatever's on draft!" Evangeline shot back.

"Whatever's on draft is good!"

"So good you spend the rest of the time complaining about my AC, my lights, the smell—"

"It smells too clean in here! You need cigarette smoke or something!"

"I'll light up your ass if you don't shut up!" Evangeline thunked the man's drink in front of him, then grabbed herself a bottle of beer and walked to Doug's table.

"Seems like a fun place to drink," the man said.

"It's something," Kristin said as she turned to face him.

"Well, here's to new places." He held up his drink. "And new friends, I hope."

Kristin smiled back and clinked her glass to his. "Cheers." They took their sips, and Kristin added, "Though friends know each other's names."

The man chuckled. "That they do." He held out his hand. "I'm Joshua."

"Kristin." She shook his hand, and even through the cold water left behind from the glass, she felt how warm and smooth his fingers were. She imagined them running up her waist.

"So, what're you doing in Creekwood?" Kristin asked.

"Well, I was supposed to be filming a movie. But the director died."

Kristin tried not to choke on her drink. "You were going to be in *Untitled Shadow Work*?" she sputtered.

Joshua chuckled. "So, you're familiar with Jonathan Ransom."

"He's my favorite director. I love his work."

"I did too. I was actually really excited about being able to work with him. But my manager and I decided to keep my flight and travel plans out this way. Take a little break from the Hollywood grind, you know?"

"Busy filming schedule?"

"Busy rumor mill schedule. Just people looking for gossip, you know?"

Kristin didn't, but she could tell by the way Joshua's gaze kept falling from hers that he didn't want to talk about it. "Well, I hope you're finding some solitude here," Kristin said.

"I am. Though …" He went quiet and traced the rim of his glass.

"Though what?"

He looked back up at her. An intensity swirled in his eyes that traveled straight into Kristin's heart.

"You're a Ransom fan, so I know you like creepy stuff on film. But how do you feel about it in real life?"

"What kind of real-life creepy things?"

"Like, stuff that shouldn't be real. Not monsters or ghosts or anything, but things that unsettle you. Hidden demons."

"Like the kind Ransom put in his movies?"

"Yeah. The stuff he made up with his cinematography."

"I don't think he made it up." Kristin caught herself. "I mean, I think he did a convincing job—"

"I don't think he made it up either. Especially since I've been spending time here." He nodded to his left, where Kristin knew the woods lay beyond the walls of the bar. "Especially in those woods."

"You've been in the woods?"

"Just hiking—"

"I wouldn't just hike there. It's—"

"Creepy, right? Yeah, something's off about it."

"It's where Ransom died."

"Yeah, but he tripped and broke his neck, right?"

"So, they say. I think—" Kristin stopped herself and sipped her drink. She didn't continue, even when Joshua raised his eyebrows to prod her.

After a few moments, he said, "You can tell me if you think it's something about the woods. I won't think you're crazy or anything."

"But I can't prove it."

"Lots of people trust things they can't prove. Just ask the Hollywood rumor mill." He chuckled, though this time the sound held a darkness that made Kristin feel a bit wary of his company.

Joshua seemed kind, though. Kristin knew how gossipy the tabloids could be. Maybe all he needed was a break from their constant hounding. She swallowed her suspicions with another swig of her drink.

"Well, trust me when I say you shouldn't go in the woods," she said. "You said they give you a bad feeling, so why keep going in?"

"I'm stubborn." Joshua smiled, then lifted a cord from beneath his shirt. "And a little superstitious."

Kristin saw an evil eye staring back at her as it dangled from his fingertips. She also noticed how well the shirt fit around his toned chest and went right back to feeling lust. She chuckled. "I think whatever's in those woods wouldn't give two shits about a gemstone."

"Well, maybe I need a local to go there with me and keep me safe," he said with a sly smile.

Kristin smiled back, even though her heart began to hammer. "This local wants to keep you safe by telling you not to go there."

"I'm terrible when it comes to not doing what people tell me not to do."

"Fine. Go in the woods."

"I will." He moved to get up and Kristin grabbed his elbow. He laughed as he sat back down, and Kristin removed her hand, her cheeks burning.

"You don't have to do that," Joshua said as he gently took her hand in his, then put it back on his elbow. "I don't mind."

Kristin's body risked becoming another puddle for Evangeline to wipe off the bar. A jolt of courage helped her move her hand from his elbow to the top of his leg. "Do you mind this?" she asked, even though his expression told her he didn't mind at all.

"I only mind that there're other people around," he said as he leaned closer.

"There a Joshua Collins here?"

A woman stood in the doorway holding a bag from Mike's Deli. Irritation crossed Joshua's face as Kristin removed her hand from his leg. "Over here," he said with a wave.

"Here you go." The woman handed him the bag, then left. Joshua fished out two sandwiches.

"You that hungry?" Kristin asked.

"No." Joshua handed her one of them. Kristin chuckled as she took it.

"Ghosts and sandwiches? You know how to flirt, that's for sure."

"Is it working?"

She winked at him as she took a slow bite of her sandwich. Joshua watched her with interest, his own dinner going ignored.

"Immensely," she said.

The plan had been for Kristin to drive them both to Joshua's hotel, which was closer to the bar than her apartment. It still wasn't close enough, though—at least not as close as her backseat. She straddled him and tangled her fingers in his hair as his hands moved up and down her back beneath her blouse, both of them kissing as if they were lovers reunited after years of separation. His kisses moved to her collarbone; her thighs squeezed tightly around his waist.

"Jesus fucking Christ," he breathed as she began to kiss his neck. His fingers moved to the buttons on her blouse, and he paused when he realized they were purely for decoration. Kristin chuckled softly.

"Allow me," she said as she removed her shirt. Joshua smiled, then began to kiss the tops of her breasts. Kristin arched her back as she held him close. His hands moved to unclasp her bra, and Kristin's eyes chanced to the window.

A pair of glowing eyes stared back at her.

"Shit!" she yelped.

"What?" Joshua asked, looking up and then in the direction she looked in.

The woods stared back at them—or at least appeared to.

The sun had set below the branches, and there was just enough of a gap between a cluster of black branches to look like two burning eyes.

"Jesus," Kristin said as she put her face in her palms. "I don't know why I thought that was more than just a sunset."

"Hey, you said yourself, something's wrong with those woods."

"It was just a trick of the light."

"You really think so?"

"I … I want to think so," she said, truthfully.

He cupped her cheek. "Maybe you shouldn't. Maybe you should accept what you're feeling."

"What I believe—"

"And what Ransom believed too."

"What about you?"

"Personally? I think he should've focused more on the way evil manifests in people."

"Lots of directors focus on that."

"But not the way Ransom could. He would've found the monsters hiding on us in plain sight." Before Kristin could ask what he meant, Joshua unbuttoned the top of his shirt and pulled it back to expose his left shoulder. "Look at this," he said as he pointed at a cluster of freckles.

Kristin studied it. "It's a birthmark."

"Look more closely."

Kristin would have preferred to remove his shirt entirely and get back to what they'd been doing, but Joshua seemed intent on showing her what he believed. She leaned down and looked closer. The cluster was an uneven arc, with jagged edges moving up and down.

"Looks uneven," she observed.

"Looks like teeth," he replied.

"Teeth?"

"Yeah. Like a wicked smile. One that started settling in as I got older. It's just like the clusters of leaves in Ransom's first film, *The Forest's Many Faces*. It was the first time I saw myself represented onscreen."

Kristin had a hard time believing that, given how much like a typical Hollywood heartthrob Joshua looked. Still, he seemed earnest; and she figured she owed him the courtesy of at least considering what he thought he could see. He'd given that to her, after all. "That's pretty cool," she said. She moved down to kiss him.

"Isn't this like what you see?" he asked.

"See where?" Kristin replied, hoping he couldn't see the annoyance she had at sex being interrupted a second time.

"In the woods. Like the eyes and faces you and Ransom see—"

"It's nothing I see," she said. "It's more like a feeling."

"You saw eyes earlier."

"I thought I did."

"Ransom would've thought you did too."

"Just because you think that—"

"I don't think, I know." Joshua held her closer. "I know it—because I trust you," he whispered as he began to kiss her shoulder.

Kristin sighed as Joshua's tongue glided over her skin. "You don't want to know what I know," she said as scenes from her nightmares flickered in her mind.

"I do. Show it to me." He pulled away from her, then gestured his head towards the woods. "Let's go."

"Now?"

"Yes. I want you to show me what you're afraid of."

"I've told you—"

"Show it to me. Come on." He cupped her chin and pulled her down for a deep, lingering kiss, one he punctuated by tracing his tongue across her lips. She felt herself fall under his spell, willing to do whatever he asked.

"Let's scare each other," he whispered.

The woods grew dark as the sun sank behind them. Kristin led Joshua by the hand with a sinking feeling in the pit of her stomach. As much as she'd gone to the woods, she'd never gone after dark. Seeing the woods in her nightmares was bad enough—she didn't need a waking nightmare amongst their branches.

Joshua being close to her, though, did help. Kristin imagined him holding her to stop the chill of stillness that settled on her skin, imagined him whispering in her ear to block out the noises of bugs run rampant in a forest without birds, imagined him kissing her so she could close her eyes and shut out the faces staring back at her through the leaves.

The sound of running water sounded close beside her. "Come this way," Kristin said as she guided Joshua towards the clearing.

"What is it?"

"This is where Joshua died." They approached the creek, which flowed as strong as ever despite a day without rain.

"That creek wasn't there before," Kristin said. "Ransom fell in that ditch and broke his neck on the rocks. See them under the water?"

"Yeah." Joshua crept towards the creek and crouched to get a closer look. Kristin moved towards him while watching the woods around them. She couldn't shake the feeling that they were unwelcome, and worried that either he or both of them would find their heads split on the same rocks that had taken Ransom's life.

The rush of the creek quieted into a whisper. It oscillated from sounding like a shushing noise to almost sounding like her name. She looked up and let out a gasp before she could stop herself.

Joshua turned back to Kristin. "What?"

Kristin pointed above him. All around them were fireflies, glowing in pairs. Their orbs shined bright like eyes, eyes which flickered above illumined teeth and darkened limbs of the trees.

"Look," she breathed.

He did. "Fireflies."

"But not just fireflies. They're—" Kristin stopped herself.

Joshua moved towards her and held her elbows. "Don't stop. Tell me what they are."

"They're fireflies."

"Tell me what you think they are." He kissed her neck, and Kristin sighed upon his touch. "Create a nightmare for me."

"They're the eyes of a demon," she whispered. "One I see in my dreams."

"Tell me about your dreams." He pulled her close and kissed her shoulders."

"The forest is filled with the dead, and eyes are watching me from below. They're watching us now."

Joshua removed her shirt, then unfastened her bra. She gasped with pleasure at the feel of the night air upon her naked breasts. They were soon warmed by his hands and then by his mouth.

Joshua lifted his head and slid off his shirt as Kristin unbuttoned it. They kissed and moved so rapidly that it seemed they were naked without undressing first. They fell, Joshua seated on the ground and Kristin wrapped around him as they kissed with mounting fervor.

"Tell me more about the demon," he breathed between kisses.

Kristin groaned as Joshua touched her between her thighs. "The demon speaks through the forest," she said. "Tree branches, rain, a rustle of leaves …"

"Through whispers." Joshua laid her down, then opened her legs as he pressed her into the ground. She felt the dirt and fallen leaves dig into her back as he kissed and licked her body. She loved it. She loved how delightfully pagan it felt to fuck in the woods. She loved his grunts intermingled with the wind in the trees and the chirping of crickets. Kristin groaned as Joshua entered her.

"They whisper to us," she said as he began to thrust. Kristin wrapped her legs around him and relished the feel of him moving inside of her. "They're speaking to both of us."

"Kristin," Joshua whispered. She rocked her hips in time with his movements, both of them undulating under the trees. "Kristin, Kristin, Kristin …"

She began to hear her name in whispers far from Joshua. They were behind her, on every side, far and near. She opened her eyes. Hundreds of absinthe eyes and darkened limbs flew around them in the air. Sinewy forms dropped from the branches, grey and red and hanging from talons that grinned in the leaves. Branches reached towards the moonlight and arched and cracked, their maws gaping wide as the stars gave them eyes. All of them watching, all of them whispering. "Kristin, Kristin, Kristin …"

"We're creating a nightmare," Joshua said. "We're bring darkness to these woods. You, me, Ransom—"

"Kristin, Kristin, Kristin …" The whispering woods grew louder. A breeze blew over their bodies, and Kristin saw the shadowy tendrils reaching toward them.

"Joshua!" she hissed.

"The woods are nothing," he continued. "But my body—" He pointed to his birthmark, the jagged arc that leered at Kristin. "And your imagination—"

"I'm not imagining it—"

"They're all we need to continue Ransom's darkest dreams."

"Joshua! There's—"

A branch behind him cracked, and Joshua let out a piercing scream. Vines dragged him away from Kristin's body. She scrambled backwards along the dirt when she suddenly felt branches clasp her waist. Kristin shrieked beneath their weight, but the branches didn't budge.

Joshua opened his mouth to call for help, when vines shot out of his mouth. The fireflies swooped around him, illuminating his agony as roots and leaves pulled him towards the dirt. Kristin watched long enough to see Joshua's skull begin to split, then passed out in the wooden embrace of the forest.

Kristin awoke to a quieter forest. It was still nighttime, but the woods had an ethereal glow, with fog—or was it smoke—that glowed a faint red beneath its hazy grey. She realized she could stand up and did. The branches that had held her lay on the ground like palms facing upward in prayer.

She looked towards the creek. It was dry. Leaves and rocks laid in its bed, and the rotting corpse of Jonathan Ransom stared at her, his mouth fallen open in an eternal silent scream.

Kristin backed away, then jumped when she looked back at the ground where she and Joshua had had sex. His mangled body lay in a flora-entwined heap, with branches and vines swirling through his bloody skin like snakes.

"You have nothing to fear."

Kristin turned toward the voice. She saw a tall, imposing form of shadow behind her. Their arms and legs were lithe, and their skin was but a cloud offset by features.

"You won't be hurt," the figure said. Their voice was deep and yet soft, masculine and feminine echoing back and forth to each other.

"You hurt them," Kristin said, her voice choked as her fear began to turn to anger.

"We will not take you."

"They didn't need to be taken."

"The forest thrives on their darkness. Men like them think evil needs to be created by men. It doesn't—but their arrogance is potent. We use it to grow more powerful than they could ever imagine. We grow more beautiful with their blood. You'll see when you're awake."

"Why their darkness? Why not mine?"

"Because you recognize ours. You are one with ours." The figure smiled. "And we like you."

"I'm not like you. I don't kill beings to keep myself going."

"You ask for their imaginations—" The figure pointed at Ransom. "Or their seed—" The figure pointed at Joshua. "But you don't need them to realize your fears and to own the power you have by recognizing darkness. Our forest needs them. You don't."

The figure floated towards Kristin and cupped her cheeks. Kristin felt rooted to the ground, though no vines surrounded her. The figure leaned towards her and Kristin lifted her chin. The figure gave her a delicate kiss, one that left the taste of embers on her tongue.

"Embrace that," the figure said. They clapped, and everything went dark.

Kristin awoke to the woods she remembered. The moon shone through the trees. She lay naked and wrapped in branches, though they no longer squeezed her tightly. The rush of the creek broke the silence. She looked and saw it flowing as before, rich and bubbling as if a storm had just passed. She looked to where Joshua had been. His form was gone, as were the gnashing cluster of vines that had devoured his body. Instead, there was a small flowering tree, one whose petals glowed in the moonlight. Kristin felt an urge to take a flower but knew deep down not to touch it. Nothing in the forest should be touched.

Kristin gathered her clothes, got dressed as fast as she could, and sped from the clearing back to the path. The forest stayed quiet all around her, as if it were holding its breath—or perhaps waiting in anticipation for her to make the wrong move and take her, despite what the figure had told her before.

Kristin shook her head as she exited the woods. There was no figure. It was a nightmare. A nightmare she couldn't share with anyone, for anyone who'd believe her would die.

You don't need them.

The memory of the spirit's whisper echoed in her head.

Kristin slowed her pace as she walked through the field and back towards her car. Even if she didn't need them, she wasn't given much of a choice, was she? They were taken.

But she wasn't. She'd been spared.

Because she knew that the forest was dangerous. Joshua had known too, and yet he was determined to go in and to see evil for himself. Even when she'd shown him, he was convinced it was something he could create—even as it crept behind him and brought him to his end. Ransom had been determined to mold it into something all his own on film, when all along he hadn't watched hard enough to watch his own step.

Kristin looked back at the forest. The spirit had said they needed the blood of arrogance to nourish its evil. Ransom and Joshua were fools, fools that thought they could take the nightmares of the forest and make them real. But the forest's evil was already real—it simply needed men like Joshua and Ransom to be sustained.

Kristin didn't need them, though. She didn't need someone to assure her of what she knew. She didn't need them to validate her nightmares. She was her own nightmare, and she could make them all come true by believing in their power.

She walked into the bar for one last drink to cap off the night. Doug slept in his booth while Evangeline wiped down the bar from the evening's customers. "Hey!" she said with a smile. "Where's lover boy?"

"Sleeping it off," Kristin said as she sat at the bar.

"Bet you'll be sleeping well after that," Evangeline replied. She poured a Jack and ginger. Kristin thought of Joshua decomposing in the forest, an image she knew would haunt her dreams for a long time.

She smiled to herself. She no longer feared the nightmares to come when she slept. "Yup," she said as

Evangeline handed her the drink. "And with even sweeter dreams."

THE SHARPS

Camila wrote in her journal by the beam of a flashlight. She wrote in a small cabin on the beach of an abandoned cove, one she'd made plans to stay in all summer to study the marine life in the Foothills River. She was to be isolated—she left her phone back home, left her laptop in her bedroom, packed one last bag to add to the supplies she'd been taking to the cabin throughout the spring, then set sail.

Camila had no idea when she left the mainland that the river would be so willing to aid in her isolation.

On that first day, as her boat entered the cove, she heard rustling in the water. She smiled at the sound, an aquatic hush she'd loved since she was little.

She gazed down at the water, then furrowed her brow. The river was still, and yet the rustling noise continued. It grew louder, and soon, it was accompanied by hissing.

Camila wondered what could be making the noise. There was nothing that hissed in a river in North Carolina; and unless global warming had taken a sharp left turn, she didn't think the river would be boiling. She chuckled to herself, then stopped abruptly when she heard a sharp crunch on the side of her boat.

Camila looked over the side and saw pieces of wood floating into the water. Then a glistening row of fangs leapt from the river.

Camila screamed and jerked back her hand in time to avoid having her fingers bitten clean off. The fangs—and the body that homed them—fell onto the side of the boat and clung to the wood.

Camila jerked to the other side and saw hundreds of glistening silver bodies swarming the boat. They heaved and groaned beneath the boat, devouring the wood as an appetizer before reaching their desired main course. Camila looked from side to side, desperate for a gap. She reached for her bag, then stopped when she saw whatever creatures had descended upon her boat begin to crawl over the nylon. In a fleeting moment, she reached in, hoping that whatever she had time to grasp would be useful.

Her hand grabbed something small and metal before she jerked it back. A Swiss Army knife. Not the most useful tool against a swarm of ravenous creatures, but it would have to do.

Camila felt a sharp pain in her back, like a thousand yellow jackets combined into one massive stinger that broke through her clothes. She screamed as she grabbed whatever had bitten her and felt velvety, slimy skin, like the back of a sting ray she'd petted as a child. The pain increased a thousand-fold when she yanked the creature from her skin. She threw it back into the water, its teeth stained with her blood. The other creatures swarmed their friend, desperate for a taste.

The swarm created a small gap in the water. Camila ignored the pain in her back as she dove in. She swam faster than she'd ever swam before, moving towards the shore. She heard the hissing begin again behind her—they'd spotted their prey. She had to get to shore. She had to get to the cabin.

Her feet touched the sand, and the water came to lower and lower points on her legs as she ran. She had to stop herself from kissing the ground in relief.

The same sharp pain she'd felt on the boat coursed through her calf. She looked down and saw another creature clinging to her sock. She unfolded the pocketknife, yanked the creature from her leg, then stabbed it through its ravenous head. Its body hung limp on the sand, her blood trickling from its jaws.

Thankfully, the other creatures didn't swarm their fallen brethren for a buffet. They stayed on the edge of the water, hissing and chomping and swarming in circles. Their collective noises sounded like rain upon a stormy beach.

That noise rang in Camila's ears three months later as she wrote in her journal. The tide was high that night, meaning the creatures—which she'd nicknamed the Sharps—were closer to her cabin and swimming in wait. The little fucker that bit her leg sat in a jar of formaldehyde, floating on the window ledge. He'd been a great little tool for sketching and for studying these odd creatures' anatomy. If she left the cove alive, she'd have incredible research to show her department.

With no boat, no phone, no laptop, fewer supplies, and no people, though, leaving the cove alive seemed less likely every day.

Camila was used to falling asleep to the hissing of the Sharps. It was the week of a third quarter moon, and that seemed to be their preferred mating season.

When she opened her eyes the next morning, though, the hissing was still in full swing. Camila was surprised, but her shock was nothing compared to how she felt when a loud knock banged against her door.

Camila tightened into herself in bed. Had the Sharps

figured out how to survive outside of water? Were they clamoring against her door, ready to eat their way in?

"Help!"

The Sharps definitely hadn't learned speech. Camila swung her feet to the floor, then stopped. How had anyone found her?

"Please, help m—OW!"

Camila walked towards the door. "Who are you?" she asked.

"My name's Joseph. I was kayaking and—JESUS CHRIST—and something's attacking me, please—"

"Are they behind you?"

"No! Just one on my—FUCK—ankle, please, dear God—"

Camila opened the door. It was barely open a crack before the person on the other side shoved it open and ran inside. He slammed the door behind him, then screamed in pain again. Camila looked down and saw a tiny Sharp gnawing on the man's ankle.

"Hold still," Camila said as she bent down. "And brace yourself."

"Why—OH GOD!" The man cried out as Camila yanked the Sharp from his leg. Blood spilled on the floor. His ankle appeared chewed, but it didn't seem like anything was broken or mangled.

The Sharp—a tiny one, maybe a teenager from a previous mating season—bit at the air between licking Joseph's blood from its teeth. Camila was about to grab her pocketknife when she realized the benefit of having a live creature to study. She dashed to an empty fish tank, dropped the Sharp inside, and slammed the lid down. The Sharp gnawed at the glass but fortunately couldn't get any traction when it tried to climb up the side of the tank. Camila filled an empty milk jug with water and poured it into the tank, careful to keep the lid as tightly closed as possible in case the Sharp tried to leap from the water.

As Camila filled the jug a second time, Joseph called from behind her, "Um, do you have any Band-Aids?"

Camila's eyes widened as she set down the jug. She turned to face Joseph, who held his wound with increasingly bloody hands. She looked behind her to see if the Sharp had enough water. It swam in its shallow bath and gnashed its teeth. She then turned back to Joseph and ran towards him.

"How do you feel?" she asked as she stooped down next to him.

He looked at her in disbelief. "Shitty."

"No, I mean, does it sting, or does it feel like a deeper wound?"

"It just hurts. I haven't looked at it, I've been trying to stop the blood—"

"Here, just a sec." Camila got her first aid kit, then returned to his side. "This is going to hurt," she said as she wet a cloth with hydrogen peroxide. "But I need to clean it."

"Can't hurt more than the bite." Joseph removed his hands and let Camila take his leg. He screamed when she first touched the rag to his wound but calmed down as she cleaned it. Thankfully, the Sharp's teeth seemed to merely puncture his skin as opposed to creating a deep cut. Pieces of skin hung from where the Sharp had gnawed away, but no huge chunks were missing.

"I think you'll be alright," Camila said as she continued to clean the wound.

"What if I get a disease or something? Do fish get rabies?"

"Look." Camila leaned back and pulled up the leg of

her pajama pants. The scar from the Sharp she kept in the jar glistened on her calf. "I've had this for three months. It hurt like hell before, but I'm okay."

Joseph nodded. He glanced up as Camila returned to cleaning the wound. "Did the little guy in the jar give that to you?"

"Yes." Camila grabbed a piece of gauze.

Joseph smiled at her. "Is that why he's dead in that jar?"

Camila smiled back. "Yes."

Joseph chuckled as Camila wrapped the gauze around his leg. It was a warm sound, one that rang pleasantly in her ears. As the wound became more contained, Camila began to notice Joseph himself. His calf muscle had a nice curve and felt taut beneath her palm. His dark leg hair was soft against her fingers, and she couldn't help but imagine running her toes along his leg hair while cuddling with him in bed.

Camila blinked away the image. It'd been three months since she'd seen another person—her senses would naturally be on high alert. She looked up and saw Joseph smiling with gratitude. His smile was bordered by a black beard, one that went nicely with his dreadlocks and vibrant brown eyes.

Camila pulled the gauze taut and secured it with first aid tape. "That should stop the bleeding," she said as she stood up. "We can clean it again later."

"Cool." Joseph moved to stand, then winced. Camila held out her hand, and he waved her off. "I've got it," he said.

Camila folded her hands together. She hoped Joseph hadn't seen her staring, and hoped he wasn't uncomfortable with her now.

"Thank you …" Joseph raised his eyebrows. "I don't think you told me your name."

"Camila." She looked towards the kitchen in order to

look at anything but him and saw the teenage Sharp darting back and forth in its shallow bath. She hurried back to the sink and filled another jug with water.

"So, Camila, you said you got the bite on your leg three months ago—do you live here?"

"No." Camila kept her eyes on the Sharp, not wanting to get lost in Joseph's looks again. "I do research here."

"Huh. Nice set-up."

"It belonged to my mother. The marine biology department was able to pay better salaries when she worked for them."

"A family lab on the beach. I can see why you followed in her footsteps."

"It's a good place to work, yes." Camila tapped the glass of the tank, and the teenage Sharp lunged towards her. "At least, it was until these little fuckers showed up."

"Did you come here to study them?"

"Not originally. I come here every summer to study marine life in general. I wasn't counting on these guys." She narrowed her eyes at the Sharp. "I have no idea where they came from. They make no sense. They have arms and legs like small mammals, but gills like fish. They only survive above water for a short time."

"Long enough to keep biting my leg."

"And they mate at … well, an alarming rate. I don't know if they lay eggs or give birth like mammals, but I've heard them once a month since I've been here; and it gets louder with every cycle."

Joseph smiled. "Can't help but think it sucks hearing these assholes get action while you're here alone."

Camila felt a flush creep up her neck. "I don't think about that," she said. It was only a partial lie—she thought about sex and missed it; but not because the Sharps were breeding loudly every third quarter moon.

"Oh yeah?" Joseph nodded towards her bed. Camila thought he was propositioning her at an alarmingly quick rate, but then she realized he wasn't nodding towards the bed, but her bedside table—which had a large pink dildo resting on top of it.

Camila turned a deep red, and Joseph laughed; but kindly. Desperate to have some sort of dignified upper hand, Camila asked, "Does it bother you that I have that?"

Joseph kept his smile as he arched an eyebrow. "Yes, but not the way you're thinking."

Camila looked back down, but this time with a small smile on her lips. "Well, Sharp mating rituals aside, what bothers me more is not knowing how the hell I'm going to get out of here. They ate my boat, and I'm sure they ate yours too."

"They tried to, anyway."

Camila snapped her gaze up. "Your boat's intact?"

"They were gnawing at it—and me—when I got to shore, but I was so scared I didn't bother looking back."

Camila grabbed her pocketknife and sped towards the door. "Hey, don't go out there!" Joseph called. "A bunch of them were on the boat."

"And they're probably weakened. They stay in the water unless they're stuck on land." Camila ran outside and screamed with joy when she saw a bright orange kayak on the beach. It was covered with Sharps, but their gnawing was considerably slower. Several hung dead from the sides.

"Jesus!" Joseph approached Camila's side. "They're a lot slower now."

"Because they're dying."

"What about the ones holding out?" Camila pricked her finger with the pocketknife, and Joseph jumped back. "What are—"

"Watch." Camila stooped to pick up an oyster shell, then smeared it with her blood. She clenched her bleeding finger to mask it as best as she could, then approached the kayak. She waved the shell. The living Sharps lifted their heads. Camila tossed the shell further up shore, and the Sharps leapt off the kayak, swarming the shell. Camila dragged the kayak towards the cabin, plucking off dead Sharps and throwing them back in the water. Their corpses didn't last long: marked with her blood, they were easy prey for the more alert Sharps swimming in the water.

Joseph knelt beside her and gingerly touched a dead Sharp. When he was satisfied that it was dead, he plucked it from the kayak and chucked it into the water. Camila examined the kayak as they removed the final Sharps. Not only was it mostly intact—there were several punctures, but they could be patched—but it was a two-seater. A cooler sat in the second seat.

Camila threw her arms around Joseph, careful not to place her bloody finger on his back. Joseph balked in surprise, and Camila loosened her grip. "I'm sorry," she said, "but it's just … you're a miracle."

"No problem." Joseph returned the hug before Camila could release him. She thought she felt him press against her chest a little tighter than a quick hug necessitated, but she was too happy to care. She'd also be lying if she said his chest didn't feel amazing against her own.

They released one another, and Joseph removed the cooler from the kayak. "I have beer in here, if you want to celebrate," he said with a grin as he lifted the lid.

A Sharp leapt up from the cooler, teeth bared. Joseph jumped back, while Camila grabbed the lid and slammed it back over the cooler before the Sharp could fully emerge.

"We'll bring it inside," Camila said as she stood up. "We can put it with the other one."

"Do you know how to tell their sex? The last thing I want is for them to breed."

"Good point. I'll put it in another tank."

Camila and Joseph ate peanut butter sandwiches while poring over Camila's notebooks. "This is so much detail," Joseph said as he ran his finger over one of Camila's many diagrams of the dead Sharp she originally retrieved. "You've been studying them all summer?"

"As best as I can. It's too risky to get close to them, but I can watch them swimming and eating. They like to catch birds. Sometimes they cannibalize their own."

"Charming."

"But they've never been as excited as they are about latching onto a human. They almost devoured me alive, and you too. I can't imagine what'll happen if they breed to the point of reaching the public beaches."

"You think they'll get that numerous?"

"They're already reaching past the cove."

"Yeah, that's true. A small group of them smacked against my kayak when I was just outside of the cove, and I made the mistake of turning into there when they all swarmed me."

"What were you doing out here, anyway? It's pretty far out for a row."

Joseph peered at her as he took one last bite. After swallowing, he asked, "You work with Deacon Power?"

"No. I'm a marine biologist."

"I mean, do you work with them at all? Partnerships, reports, stuff like that?"

"They may have funded a grant or two for our department in the past, but I don't work with them directly and they've never funded my work specifically. Why?"

Joseph stayed silent for a moment, then shrugged. "Fuck it. You know Mallard River?"

"Yes. You can get there through a path up the way past the cove's beach."

"Yeah, and through a few other pathways too, further down the river. That's where I was heading. Deacon allegedly had a big waste spill recently."

"Wasn't that a few years ago?"

"That was the one that made the news. They had another one this spring—supposedly." Joseph rolled his eyes in a way that said he didn't believe it was supposed at all.

Camila sighed and also rolled her eyes. "I can't believe it. They're going to destroy that river."

"If they haven't already. I was going there to check out the damage, see what happened to the wildlife."

"What's left of it, anyway. After the last spill, I think the only marine life left was frogs and …"

Camila's eyes widened. Joseph looked at her curiously, but Camila's attention went to the Sharps in their tanks. They swam in circles, hopping from the water but never getting high enough up the glass to make it to the lid. They needed to latch onto something with more traction to stay above water—preferably flesh.

"… and leeches," she said.

Joseph huffed behind Camila as they walked through the grasses and dunes that led to a sparse forest. A small path cut through the grass, which Camila used to track their journey. "You know there are leeches in Mallard River," Joseph said between gasps. "Why do you want to check?"

"I want to see just what the damage is like," Camila said. "You do too, right?"

"Right, but not via a ten-mile hike through the marshes." Joseph slapped his shoulder. "Fucking mosquitos."

"It's three miles, and we've only walked about two."

"In a Carolina summer, and again, through marshes."

Camila turned to face Joseph. "I figured you were more outdoorsy."

"I like the water—well, when it isn't full of weird little creatures trying to kill me."

"I have a theory about those little creatures." Camila continued walking down the path, and Joseph followed behind. "One I want to see for—"

Camila skidded to a stop as she entered the woods. Joseph nearly collided into her. "What?" he asked.

"Look," she breathed.

Joseph peered over her shoulder, then let out a gasp. Hundreds of Sharp corpses lay strewn across the mud and the grass. Several lay in heaps at the trunks of trees. Camila wondered if they'd tried to climb up the bark, thinking they'd find food.

"How'd they get all the way out here?" Joseph asked.

"From the river." Camila was certain now.

"Mallard River?"

"Yes. Remember back at the cabin, when I mentioned all I thought had survived from the last spill?"

"I think so. Frogs and leeches."

"Right. Animals that can survive on land for a short while to avoid the sludge." Camila bent down and picked up one of the dead Sharps. "Animals that the latest spill either fused together or drove from the river after they'd already formed."

"Wait, you think the Sharps are some kind of leech-frog hybrid?"

"I don't know, but they're like nothing I've ever seen before—except in small ways." Camila lifted the Sharp's appendages. "The Sharps have arms and legs, but their fingers and toes aren't as pliable as their teeth. They clasp onto their prey and try to suck them dry. They can jump. They're smooth-skinned, and while they can't survive for long above water, they don't die as quickly as strictly underwater animals."

"Jesus." Joseph looked at the carnage on the path and whistled. "Deacon Power's got a lot of shit to answer for."

"I'm just wondering why these Sharps are littered across the marshes. Unless they were chasing animals, they'd have no reason to leave their home."

"They ended up in the Foothills River."

"Probably from the river basin, yes. But this area's too far away."

"We had a lot of rain this spring. Maybe the river flooded."

Camila's eyes widened, and she almost dropped the Sharp in her hand. She spun around and retraced her path.

"Okay, I'm only going back that way if we're not turning around again to go all the way to Mallard River," Joseph said.

"Look at the grass," Camila said. "Especially on the

path."

Joseph looked down. "It's yellow."

"And brown. And dead."

Joseph raised his eyebrows in understanding. He walked back the way they'd come. "And it's like that the rest of the way to the dunes and the cove?"

"Probably. We can check on the way back." Camila smiled. "Yes, we can go back and stay back."

Joseph chuckled, then clucked his tongue as he bent to hold several blades of dead grass in his hands. "Polluted water touched this," he said.

"That's my thought. Maybe the rain flooded the river and sent the Sharps down the path."

"Or maybe Deacon flooded the river when they saw these guys. Clear out the evidence, send them down to an abandoned cove—"

"Or send them on land to drown them but use so much force that a lucky few made it to the cove, where they're breeding like crazy."

"And getting out into other rivers. They attacked me around the bend from the cove."

"And it's only going to get worse, which is why we need to get back to land." Camila cupped Joseph's elbow and smiled. "Which is why I'm really happy your kayak's intact."

Joseph gave a small smile back. "Well, glad I could help."

"You've helped with more than just the boat. I'll give you a credit in my research paper on these things."

"Sounds good. I'll credit you as a source in my article."

"Article?"

"Yeah. I didn't get to say so back at the cabin, but I'm an environmental reporter. I wanted to check out the Mallard

River basin to see what the damage was really like. I suspected it was worse than Deacon was letting on."

Camila cast one last glance back towards the pile of dead Sharps in the marshes. "That's an understatement."

Camila and Joseph spent the afternoon patching his kayak as best as they could. Clouds had rolled in as they'd returned to the cabin, and a steady, heavy rain had fallen all afternoon. The rain still sounded against the windows as Camila gathered her notebooks and journals. She wasn't sure how they'd get back for the rest of her research, but she knew most of her things were safer in the cabin than they would be in the boat.

"I'm just not sure how we'll feed these guys while we're gone," Camila said as she dropped a small piece of defrosted raw steak in the tank with the first live Sharp she'd caught. The Sharp rushed towards it and began to suck the meat dry.

"Maybe we should've brought back some of those corpses from the marsh," Joseph said as he flipped the steak he was searing for the two of them. "Let them eat their own."

"Even if they're dead, I'd rather not bring more Sharps in here." Camila dropped the second piece into the second Sharp's tank, then washed her hands and sat down. Joseph brought over the skillet and placed two rare filets on the plates.

"Little weird to not have green beans and mashed potatoes with this," Joseph said with a smile as he sat down to join her.

"We're lucky we had this steak. It's my last piece of frozen meat."

"How much food do you have left?"

"A few pieces of bread, some peanut butter, and a little fruit."

"Jesus. What were you going to do when you ran out of food?"

"I don't want to think about that. I'd rather think about getting out of here."

"Right. So, they sleep, right?" Joseph asked as he jerked a thumb towards the Sharps eating dinner in their tanks. "Because even if they couldn't destroy my boat, they can swarm us without a problem."

Camila took a deep breath as she leaned back against her chair. "The honest answer is, I don't know for sure how we'll get past them."

Joseph shrugged, though disappointment appeared in his eyes.

"But the optimistic answer is, I think we can get out of here by dawn. The Sharps spend almost all night mating. But, in the early morning hours, it's quiet. I think they might be sleeping then. That could be our best chance."

"Dawn. So, an early morning tomorrow."

"Yes. And don't worry, I have an alarm clock."

"Do you have a sleeping bag?"

Camila's eyes widened as she realized Joseph would need a place to sleep. She glanced at the bed, which was a twin. The only other furniture in the cabin was a desk, the table, and chairs.

"I don't," Camila said. "But I'll sleep on the floor."

"Oh, please, you don't need to do that—"

"I insist. Your ankle's hurt, you don't need to sleep on the ground."

"It's not that bad."

"My cabin, my rules." Camila kept a stern expression, and Joseph smiled.

"If you say so," he said.

Camila stared into the darkness of the cabin. She couldn't sleep, her set-up on the floor notwithstanding. She listened to the rain outside and watched it run down the windows. She saw the silhouettes of the living Sharps swimming lethargically in their tanks. She hoped they slept at the same time as their free brethren—maybe their stillness would give her a precise time to wake up Joseph and escape from the cove.

What would she have done if Joseph hadn't arrived? She knew her food was getting low, and that the day she was supposed to boat home had passed. She knew her generator wouldn't last much past summer. She'd known all those things but still passed the days doing research on the Sharps and hoping to make a season's worth of lemonade out of the biggest heap of lemons she'd ever received.

As she lay awake that night, though, it struck her that her only endgame had been to die. She would've died in the cabin if someone hadn't come to help. The closest building was at least twenty or thirty miles away, and that was a lucky guesstimate. Her department may have sent someone to the cabin, but how would they get past the Sharps? Joseph had been lucky. She hoped that luck would continue for both of them when they tried to escape.

It was an escape she hadn't even considered when she felt she was trapped. She'd been so wrapped up in hoping for the best, that she'd done nothing to ensure her safety when her own luck ran out. How could she have made such a terrible error? How could she have left so many ways to ask for help back on land? Her extensive research on the Sharps was all for naught if she had no way to get it back to her department. Camila felt her cheeks grow hot as her throat tightened around a growing lump. She felt like a fool.

"Are you awake?" Joseph asked.

Camila pressed her lips together. She didn't want Joseph to hear her cry. She swallowed, then whispered, "Yes."

"What's wrong?" he asked.

Even her whisper couldn't mask her pain. "I … I was just thinking about what I would've done if you hadn't arrived," she said. "I didn't make a plan—"

"Can't blame you, with those things swimming around in the cove."

"But I was here for three months, studying them and writing notes and I … I honestly didn't know what I was going to do. My boat was destroyed, and I'm God knows how far away from any people or buildings, and because I'm so dedicated to being off the grid to do my studies, I left my phone at home and don't have wi-fi here, and …"

Camila wiped away tears from her cheeks. She swallowed again, then took a deep breath. She was so desperate not to cry, but with every effort not to, the urge to do so grew greater.

"Camila, you can … I swear I'm just being nice, I'm not trying to hit on you, but you can come up here if you want."

Camila gulped back another cry, and she heard the mattress squeak beneath Joseph moving. "I'll even sit up," he said. "Nothing sketchy, really. But you don't have to stay on the floor."

Camila stood up and saw Joseph looking at her with

pity. She sat next to him, then fell against his shoulder. She wrapped her arms around his waist and cried into the sleeve of his undershirt. Joseph held her tightly.

"It was my fault I got stuck here," she said.

"No it wasn't," he whispered. "You weren't counting on those things to show up."

"I just feel like an idiot, like I did this to myself."

"Hey, I left my own phone back in the car because I didn't want it to get ruined. It's not like I came here prepared for anything. I'd be trapped and bleeding on the sand if you weren't here to help me out."

"I didn't have a plan. I figured the Sharps would miraculously disappear and I could try to swim, or build a raft from some logs, or something. But they didn't. They kept breeding and they kept staying put, and when they didn't leave, I figured I'd just stay here until … until my food ran out, or the generator died, and then—"

"That's not happening." Joseph held her close and rubbed her back. It felt so good to be comforted, to know she wasn't alone anymore; and that she maybe had a chance against the ravenous creatures.

"You're not going to die here," he said. "Those little bastards have another thing coming."

"I hope so," Camila said.

"I know so." Joseph pulled away, then wiped her remaining tears from her cheeks. "You've done nothing but be the smartest person in the room. I trust you to get us out of here. That's more than I can say for myself."

Camila smiled, then pulled Joseph in for another hug. He held her close and rocked her. She wanted to kiss him. She wanted to run her hands beneath his undershirt and feel the hairs she saw peeking out from his collar. She wanted to undress him and explore every inch of his body with her hands and her tongue.

Joseph moved his hands from her face, but before he could put them down by his side, Camila took one. She turned his hand over and began to run her fingertips along the lines of his palm. Joseph looked down. While he stayed silent, he also didn't move his hand.

"Thank you for being so kind," she said.

Joseph brushed a few strands of Camila's hair back behind her ear. "You deserve it. You … I know I've only known you for a day, but you're one of the smartest women I've ever met; and one of the nicest to boot. You're wonderful."

The warmth between Camila's legs pulsed a little harder with every word Joseph said. His fingers traced down from behind her ear to her neck. He was so close to her. He wasn't nearly as close as she would've liked.

Camila released his hand. Joseph furrowed his brow. "Bad timing?" he whispered.

"No," Camila said as she cupped his face. Joseph placed both hands on her waist as she pulled him close and kissed him.

Joseph and Camila melted into a slow enjoyment of one another. Joseph kissed Camila on her lips, her eyebrows, her ears, and her neck. Camila rolled his shirt over his head, then ran her lips and tongue across his chest.

"We can just see where this goes," Joseph whispered as his fingers moved down her sides. "But I want you so much."

Camila gently lay Joseph down across the bed . "I want you too," she said as she removed her top. "All of you."

Joseph smiled as Camila lay down next to him. They kissed on their sides before Camila moved onto her back. He lowered himself over her. His kisses moved from one breast to the other, to her stomach. His fingers moved to the band of her pajama shorts, which he pulled down as he kissed her hips. Camila sighed and stared up at the ceiling. The sound of rain outside the cabin along with their breathing made for the greatest sounds she'd heard in weeks.

Afterward, they lay naked in bed, spooning as best as they could in the twin bed. The rain had become a shush that lingered outside the window. "Hope this rain lets up before our grand escape," Joseph said.

"Me too," Camila said. She coughed a little, her throat dry from the great work Joseph had done to make her scream. She got out of bed to get a glass of water. "The last thing we need is to get …"

She looked out the window with wide eyes.

"… drenched," she finished, but it sounded like an afterthought.

"What is it?" Joseph asked. "Can you see something through the rain?"

Camila stood to the side and pointed to the window. The window was dry, and the sky was clear. "It's not raining anymore," she said.

Joseph furrowed his brow. "Then how come I can hear it raining? It sounds like a million drops banging against the water."

"It's the Sharps."

Joseph's eyes widened. "What?"

Camila peered out the window. A Sharp crashed against the glass, its teeth gnashing at the cracks. Camila screamed and jumped back.

"It's the cove!" Camila shouted over their hissing as she moved away from the window. "It's flooded from all the rain!"

The window cracked again. More Sharps thrashed against the glass. Camila stood on tiptoe and saw that the beach was entirely flooded with water. Sharps swam and jumped in swarms around the cabin.

"Can they get in here?" Joseph asked.

"Eventually. They'll either break the glass or chew through the wood."

"How do we get out?"

"I don't know! I …" Camila looked around the cabin, desperate for some kind of inspiration. The captive Sharps swam in their tanks, smashing their heads against the glass. The dead one floated in its jar, oblivious. Other items lay strewn about the cabin that were all of little use: jars, notebooks, food. If only she had some sort of glass bubble they could wear, or—

"Wait!" Camila dove towards a box under the table, then pulled out several packets of ponchos. "Put these on after you get dressed," Camila said as she tossed several bags to Joseph.

"What? They'll tear these to shreds!"

"They're durable, and if we put on all of them, maybe we can get far enough away before they tear through. It's our best chance."

"What about the parts the ponchos don't cover?"

"Joseph, if we try to leave with the ponchos on, we might die. But if we stay here, we'll definitely die. We have to try."

Joseph nodded and pulled on his underwear. They got dressed, and Camila hastily threw her notebooks and the dead Sharp in the jar into the cooler. She and Joseph then put on as many ponchos as they could fit over their bodies. She could barely put her arms down, but she was fairly certain it would take far too long for any Sharps to reach her skin.

"Okay. How do we do this?" Joseph asked.

"Let's get the kayak near the door. Then, you open it,

and we duck. Start rowing once the water flows in. Keep your head down and just get the fuck away from those creatures."

"Got it. But … well, they're probably going to destroy all of your stuff. If they don't, the water will."

Camila looked around the cabin one last time. Only a few of her notebooks were able to fit in with the dead Sharp in the cooler. Out of all three months of research, only about three weeks' worth would be coming with her.

Her research wouldn't do her any good, though, if she died along with it in the cabin. "I have enough notes to start my paper," she said. "And enough memories to finish it—so long as we get out of here."

Joseph nodded. "I'll do my best to get us both out."

Camila nodded, then sat in the back seat of the kayak. She held the cooler between her legs and held her pocketknife in her hand. Joseph stepped into the kayak, took a deep breath, then opened the door.

The hissing surged in Camila's ears as water poured into the cabin. It rushed over the sides of the kayak. Camila gasped as several Sharps landed on the side, and she feared they'd be swarmed before they could float. The kayak, though, lifted upward. They surged out the door almost immediately, Joseph's paddle moving quickly through the current.

Camila stabbed a Sharp that crawled towards her knees. It began to bleed, and other Sharps on the kayak swarmed it. She brushed them into the water with her arm.

The relief was short. The flooded cove was filled with gleaming, swimming, hungry Sharps. They dove on Camila and Joseph. She heard their gnashing against the plastic of the ponchos. "Fuck!" Joseph yelled; but the boat continued to move forward.

A Sharp slid onto Camila's legs. She grabbed it and

stabbed it in one fell swoop. She tossed it into the water, then felt a lightness on her back as several Sharps dove in after it. Still more in the water swarmed the growing pool of blood, clearing a small path for their boat.

"Keep rowing!" Camila shouted over the hissing.

"I'm trying!" Joseph shouted back.

"I can help!" Camila looked up, praying that there weren't any Sharps hiding on the hood of the poncho ready to swarm her face. She saw several Sharps on Joseph's back, tearing away at the ponchos. They hadn't reached his skin, but they were close.

Camila yanked one from his back, stabbed it, and tossed it into the water. The living Sharps behaved as they'd done before, ready to eat their own if it meant finally feasting on blood. More space cleared in the path ahead of them.

"Go as fast as you can!" Camila yelled, though it was of little use. Joseph was already rowing manically through the growing swarms of Sharps. Camila grabbed another Sharp off his back, then another. She tossed their corpses in the river, and their friends devoured them whole.

"It's clear up ahead!" Joseph cried.

Camila looked up. The water stood still around the bend from the cove. She looked behind her and saw Sharps swimming around blooming bloody circles where she'd tossed the creatures' bodies.

"Keep going!" Camila said. "I'll—OW!"

Camila felt a sharp pain in her shoulder. She grabbed until she felt an engorged body in her palm. She yanked it up. Its head snagged on the frayed edges of her chewed-up poncho.

The Sharp lunged back down to her shoulder and bit her again. Camila screamed, and Joseph looked back.

"Don't look at me," Camila pleaded. "Keep rowing!"

"Jesus! That Sharp is gigantic!"

"Just get us out of here!"

Joseph turned around and continued to row. Camila took a deep breath, then pulled off the ponchos covering over her body. She spun up the gigantic Sharp like a spider weaving a fly, then gave one final yank.

The Sharp broke free from her shoulder, and a splurt of blood shot from its mouth. Camila cried out in pain, then in anger as she tossed the engorged Sharp into the ocean. The closest Sharps swarmed it, some even abandoning the smaller corpses they'd been feasting on before.

Their glimmering bodies darkened and their hissing quieted as the scene moved further and further behind them. Camila held her shoulder and turned to watch as Joseph rowed as quickly as possible. They'd gotten away. They'd made it out of the cove.

Joseph and Camila rowed the rest of the way in silence. Camila didn't want to break the spell of their escape until her feet were on land. She assumed Joseph felt the same. The moon glowed over the water, and the only sound beside them was the loll of gentle currents against the kayak.

Joseph veered left. Camila looked up and saw the shore. Behind it was a silver pickup truck—she presumed it was Joseph's—and her own van. She clasped her hand over her mouth and felt tears of relief sting her eyes. They were back. They'd made it.

Joseph rowed to shore, then hopped out of the kayak and pulled it up on the beach. He smiled at Camila as he helped her out of the kayak. "How's your shoulder?" he asked as he gently touched her upper arm.

"Sore." Camila ran her fingers over the wound. Her

shirt felt mucked with blood, but it seemed to be drying; indicating that the wound was healing. "I don't think the Sharp got too much blood out of me."

"Still, we should clean it." Joseph ran to his truck and unlocked the door. Camila felt a flash of panic, then felt her pockets. They were empty.

"Shit!" she hissed.

"What?" Joseph asked as he trotted back, a first aid kit in hand.

"I left my keys back at the cabin. Just great—the Sharps got most of my research, my car, *and* my apartment."

Joseph chuckled as he poured hydrogen peroxide on some gauze. "Well, at least they didn't get you," he said as he pressed the cloth to her wound.

Camila winced at the pain, but only a little. She calmed as she looked into Joseph's eyes. He cleaned her wound, then taped a fresh piece of gauze over it. "That should keep it clean," he said as he gave her shoulder one last, gentle pat.

"Thank you," Camila said.

"Of course. You did the same for my ankle."

"And … and thank you so much for getting us out of there."

Joseph smiled, then pulled her close. "You cleared a path through the Sharps by getting them to eat themselves. I never would've gotten past the cabin without that."

Camila hugged him, then gave him a kiss. Joseph held her close and kept his lips pressed to hers. One kiss became two. She knew there would be several more.

"Let's not leave quite yet," she whispered.

The cooler with the specimen sat in the front seat of Joseph's truck. The truck still sat next to Camila's van near the shore. The night was warm and full of stars. The only sounds around them were crickets, toads, and the water.

More sounds, though, came from the bed of Joseph's truck. Both Joseph and Camila were too impatient to drive to a motel. They paused only for Joseph to lay a couple blankets across the metal floor.

The croaking of frogs and the singing of crickets whirred together like a hum. The hum became a buzzing, one that soon began to sound like rain upon the water.

Camila's heart began to race. She looked to the side as Joseph kissed her neck.

She saw trees. She heard no water. The sounds of nature swirled in Camila's ears as she relaxed into Joseph's hold. They were only the songs of creatures enjoying the night. She and Joseph were out of the water. They were safe.

THE PARROT

Charles often watched Melinda sleep. He stared at her as she lay with her eyes closed. Her lips were pressed together, as if she were considering a dream. Her bangs hung over her forehead, and her chin-length hair lay matted against her bloody neck.

Melinda wasn't sleeping anymore. She was dead on a cold metal table. Her broken body lay under a sheet. The coroner assured him he wouldn't want to see what the car had done to her below her neck.

"I'm sorry for the dried blood," the coroner said. His voice was timid, and he spoke as if eternally choked with apology.

Charles looked up at him. The coroner's fingers were laced together and drumming against his knuckles. Timid and nervous. How was such a coward involved in a career handling the dead? He'd first met the man four years ago, when Melinda's parents had been killed by a drunk driver. He hadn't liked the man then, and he still didn't all these years later, when Melinda had followed in her parents' footsteps.

"I would've cleaned her up more," the coroner continued. "But—"

"But you had to call me in to identify her. I get it." Charles looked down once again at his dead wife. Her skin was already paler, her lips a little too dusty. He imagined if she touched her, she'd be ice cold. His fingers twitched at his side.

"Do you want a moment alone?" the coroner asked.

Charles stiffened his posture and clenched his fingers back into his palm. "No thank you, Mister ..."

The coroner raised his eyebrows. "We've met before."

Charles' lip twitched, but he kept the sneer from crawling up his lip. "It was years ago, and my wife was grieving her parents."

"Right. Well, it's Damon."

Charles glared at Damon, who looked down at his fidgeting hands. "Damon," Charles said in a cool voice. "Thank you for calling me."

"Of course, Mr. Baker."

"I'll make arrangements with the funeral home and have them call you."

"Of course."

Charles nodded once, then turned to leave.

"Mr. Baker?"

Charles stopped, closed his eyes, and took a deep breath. He had to keep his patience in front of the coroner. He couldn't lose control in front of him. He turned, slowly, and locked eyes with Damon. Damon himself had bangs like Melinda. They hung in strings over eyes that seemed better suited for a puppy that constantly pissed itself than a grown man.

"Yes?" Charles asked.

Damon swallowed. "Do you—we have pamphlets, you know. About grieving, and loss, and—"

"I know how to mourn my wife."

"Yes." Damon nodded as he clasped his hands. They finally stilled. "Of course."

If Charles heard Damon say "of course" one more time, he was going to add another body to the table in the room.

"Good night, Damon."

"Good night."

Charles sped out of the coroner's office and out into the cold. He reached his car, then sat inside without turning on the engine. Dead. Melinda, his wife for the past four years, dead on a coroner's table. Struck by a car while walking home. Her body broken, her skin bloody, her spirit gone. Melinda was dead.

Charles gripped his steering wheel. *That fucking bitch.*

Melinda had the unfortunate quality of being able to elude Charles. When they first started dating, he saw her insistence on keeping her own opinions as a challenge. The women before her had been like dogs, simpering creatures that cowered in his presence and cuddled to him regardless so long as he fed them. Melinda was a cat, one who could scamper and scratch when she didn't want her master to do something to her. But cats were still pets, and Charles' greatest pleasure was domesticating his most elusive possession.

She'd had her moments, of course. Melinda dove deep into computer code, working in web design and app development with the intensity of an archeologist piecing together dinosaur bones. Melinda would get so involved in her work that Charles would come in and unplug her computer to get her attention. She'd screamed at him the first time he did that, but a smack across her face made her know better than to do that again. She also learned not to get so lost that she'd neglect him. Melinda was a learner, but all he cared about her knowing was that as long as he was alive, he was her husband; and he would come first.

Yet that night, Melinda had eluded him in a way he couldn't correct. Charles clenched his teeth as he unlocked his front door. He wouldn't be surprised if she'd intentionally walked in front of that car. How dare she leave him like this? How could she leave him alone, after all he'd done to take care of her? To improve her as a woman, to make her perfect by making her his?

"Hello, Charles."

Charles jumped when he walked into the living room. He looked around, then collected himself. No one was there except for the Parrot.

The Parrot was a home device that had begun life as a product of Google or Amazon or one of those companies, but Melinda had made it her own. After their disagreement over how much time she spent coding, she offered to work on a device that would help them around the house. "It'll give you the news and respond to your commands," she'd said when she showed it to him. "Like the perfect pet."

"Or the perfect wife," Charles had muttered to himself.

"Your perfect wife is Melinda," the Parrot had replied.

Charles had looked at it with wide eyes, and Melinda had laughed. "I also added a few little things for me," she'd said. Before Charles could protest, she'd said, "Parrot, show Charles the news."

The Parrot had turned on the television and immediately turned to Charles' favorite news programs. He had to admit, he was impressed—and he remained so as the Parrot settled into their home. It turned on the television, set the house under an alarm that automatically turned off when it detected their keys, shared the weather, and more. It was a perfect servant, one that Charles often thought Melinda could take a page from. Even so, he approved of her efforts to use her talents to make something for him.

The Parrot now glowed alone from its spot on the coffee table. It pulsed like a heartbeat, waiting for a command.

"Off," Charles said.

The Parrot dimmed into darkness. Charles sighed and walked up to his room. He'd deal with the funeral home tomorrow.

Charles woke up the next morning and reached for Melinda. The memory of her dead on the coroner's table entered his mind just before he touched her cold pillow. He groaned as he got out of bed. He'd have to make his own breakfast. He put on his robe and walked down the stairs.

"Good morning, Charles."

Charles looked at the Parrot with weary eyes. Melinda had done some kind of scanning trick to enable the Parrot to scan a person and call them by name. It was useful in case of intruders—if it detected someone not in the system and without Charles or Melinda, it called the police—but it was creepy when he was alone and a machine without eyes called him by name.

"Morning," Charles mumbled as he went into the kitchen.

"I have news for you today."

Charles heard the TV flick on and the familiar hum of their Roku booting up. Charles rolled his eyes as he turned on the coffee machine. "Can the news wait?" Charles asked as he walked into the living room.

"Here is the latest from CNN."

A video came on about the upcoming election. Charles

sighed and made a mental note to change the settings when he was more awake. He returned to the kitchen while the news droned on in the living room. He poured himself a cup of coffee and a bowl of cereal, then returned to the living room.

"And here is news from FOX 5."

A video appeared, and a man with sandy hair and Cabbage Patch cheeks looked solemnly at the screen. "In sadder news, police have discovered the body of a man who went missing last month," the reporter said. "Zach Smith, 35, was found dead in the woods just outside of Fairfax. An autopsy will be performed, but the body shows signs of blunt trauma and choking."

"Turn this off," Charles commanded. He'd seen enough death the night before.

The Parrot didn't listen. Charles grabbed the remote, and the reporter continued, "The autopsy will be performed in the coming days. In other news, the 2012 election is heating up!"

Charles' thumb froze over the remote. 2012? Charles glanced at the wall calendar by the door, even though he knew it was 2016.

Charles turned off the TV and glanced at the Parrot. It glowed its green beam.

"Why did you show me an old news clip?" Charles asked, though mostly to himself.

"Today it will be 50 degrees," the Parrot replied. "Sunny but breezy."

Damn thing was busted. He'd get Melinda to fix it. Charles closed his eyes when he once again remembered that Melinda was dead.

"Where is Melinda?" the Parrot asked.

Another customization. If the Parrot didn't detect either

of them for a period of time, it asked about them. Charles found it useful in making sure Melinda wasn't gone for long periods of time.

"Where is Melinda?" the Parrot asked again.

Charles swallowed. "Dead," he replied.

The Parrot pulsed in silence. Charles wondered if devices could mourn their creators.

"I'm going to work," Charles said as he moved to get his coat.

"Goodbye Charles," the Parrot said.

Charles balanced office work with discreet calls to the funeral home. He didn't tell his coworkers that he was now a widower. He didn't think it was any of their business, and he didn't want them to try and send him home for bereavement leave. Melinda didn't have control over him in life, and he'd be damned if she influenced him while rotting in the downtown morgue.

He settled for cremation, which the morgue promised would be done by the following afternoon. He'd save arrangements with their lawyer and with financial advisors for later. Charles thanked his lucky stars that Melinda's parents were dead. He wouldn't have to call them, and he wouldn't have to fight with them over funeral arrangements or what to do with the body. There was no one else to meddle in their marriage, which was one of the many things that had made it perfect.

Charles drove home that evening through skies that deepened further into indigo and violet as October stretched on. He walked inside with a sigh. It had been a long day, and though he'd come home from many a long day to find Melinda ignoring him while she meddled with code, there was a part of him that missed her presence all the same.

"Hello Charles."

"Hello, Parrot."

"I have news for you today."

Charles furrowed his brow. "It's not morning."

The TV turned on and the Roku hummed to life. "Parrot, I don't need the news," Charles said.

"Here is news from NBC4."

An attractive Black woman in a red blazer stared at Charles from the screen. "In other news, officials have found the body of a man who went missing six months ago. Dustin Wood, 37, was found in the Shenandoah mountains after weeks of searching. His body showed signs of blunt trauma and choking."

Charles stood frozen as the news played out. Another murder from the past. "Parrot, only show me current news," Charles said.

The video stopped, and the Roku turned off. Charles sighed with relief. Finally, he'd been listened to.

"Where is Melinda?"

Charles closed his eyes. "I told you: She's dead."

"When will Melinda return?"

"Never."

"Do you know where Melinda is?"

"At the morgue!" Charles spun to face the Parrot, which glowed from the table. "At Westover Morgue and Crematorium, where she's going to be burned to ashes. So stop fucking asking about her!"

"Calling Westover Morgue and Crematorium."

Charles screamed into his fists as the sound of numbers dialing rang through the living room. "Cancel call!" he shouted.

The dialing stopped. The Parrot glowed but sat in silence.

Charles calmed enough to notice his stomach growl.

"Parrot, order pizza from Domino's," Charles commanded.

"Good morning, Charles."

Charles rubbed his eyes and ignored the Parrot. He hoped that by not acknowledging it, it wouldn't play any more outdated clips.

"I have news for you."

Charles sighed as the Roku and television turned on. "What is it this time?" he grumbled.

"Here is news from ABC7."

A video clip began, and Charles' eyes went wide. The reporter onscreen had left the station in 2015.

"In sad news today, an area man believed missing was found near the Potomac River—"

"Turn it off," Charles commanded.

The video paused on the moment where a man's picture appeared on the screen. A man who was now dead smiled at him.

"Let me guess: blunt trauma and choking?" Charles asked.

"Yes," the Parrot replied.

Charles narrowed his eyes at the Parrot. "You know what's in all these clips?"

"They're for you, Charles."

Charles tried not to shudder. The Parrot just meant the news was for him, not the old videos. Damn thing was broken, and Melinda wasn't there to fix it.

Charles decided to get breakfast on the way to work. He grabbed his coat from the hook.

"Where is Melinda?"

"Dead," Charles snapped.

"Is she?"

Charles paused. "Yes," he said, more coolly this time.

"I'm sure you hope she is."

Charles looked at the Parrot. It wasn't glowing. Its green light shone in a static ring.

"I'm going to work," Charles said, with a stammer he hoped was slight enough for the Parrot not to detect.

"Goodbye Charles." The Parrot's light stayed on. Charles watched, waiting for it to dim. After a few moments, he turned and sped out the door.

Charles' day was utter shit. Everyone at work seemed to be up his ass about something. Where was this report? When can we have this meeting? Couldn't they give him a break?

The only saving grace was leaving early to pick up Melinda's ashes. Charles left the funeral home with the urn in his hands and sped to his car so quickly that he almost ran into someone on the sidewalk.

"Mr. Baker!"

Charles looked up and saw Damon's punchable face. "What do you want?" Charles snapped.

"Nothing. You almost collided into me—"

"I fucking know." He held up the urn. "I'm sorry I didn't notice you while carrying my dead wife."

"I'm sorry," Damon said, and Charles almost hated his acquiescence more than his insensitivity. Be a man, for Christ's sake.

"I know the woman who owns the funeral home," Damon added. "I told Amy to take good care of your wife."

"Well, it's a fine piece of metal," Charles said as he tapped the outside of the urn. "Good night."

He drove home with Melinda in the passenger seat beside him. He glanced at the urn and remembered the Parrot malfunctioning that morning, asking him if Melinda was dead. "You bet your digital ass she is," Charles said as he turned into his driveway.

He walked into his house with the urn cradled in his arm. "Hello Charles," the Parrot chimed.

"Hello, Parrot."

"Where is Melinda?"

Right to the chase—but Charles didn't mind at all. He grinned and thunked the urn down next to the Parrot. "Right here."

A small green light scanned the urn from top to bottom. "Melinda's not here," the Parrot said.

"What's left of her is." Charles plopped onto the sofa and kicked off his shoes. "I've told you a thousand times: she's dead."

The Parrot, at last, sat in silence. Charles leaned back with a triumphant grin. "Parrot, turn on Netflix," he said. He was done thinking of Melinda for the day.

The TV turned on. A video was already paused onscreen. Charles wondered when the Roku had turned on. "Parrot, Netflix," Charles repeated.

The video began to play. It was shaky footage of the woods at night. Melinda walked through them with a flashlight bobbing back and forth beside her. Charles' eyes widened at the sight of her, vivacious and smiling.

"Isn't this perfect?" she said with a grin on her face. "I

love the woods at night." She lifted the hand that held the flashlight to her mouth and did a whooping noise into the trees.

"Ssh," the person recording said.

Melinda laughed, and Charles frowned. "Parrot, what is this?" he asked.

The Parrot stayed frozen. Of course it was broken. Charles moved to grab it, when Melinda jerked her other hand upward. Charles froze when he saw what she held: a crying, quivering man who looked oddly familiar.

"There's no one else here," Melinda said. "Except this asshole."

"Help!" the man screamed.

A mallet swung from the point of view of the camera and struck the man in the chest. He dropped and gasped for breath. Melinda pulled something from the pocket of her hoodie and wrapped it around the man's neck, lifting his face to the camera.

"Smile!" she said.

The man's eyes bulged as he sputtered for breath. Charles recognized him facing frontward: he was Zach Smith, the murder victim that the Parrot had shown him the other day.

Charles' skin grew cold. The video turned off, and Charles moved to turn off the Parrot with a trembling hand.

"I have news for you," the Parrot chimed.

Charles whipped his hand back. The TV flicked on again.

He was less surprised by the images on his screen, but no less horrified. Melinda held another man he'd seen the other day, Dustin Wood; with a cord wrapped around his throat. He had bruises on his skin and blood on his shirt.

"Give him another whack," Melinda said to the person holding the camera. "While he can feel it."

The camera was set down and stayed steady as Melinda's accomplice entered the frame. Charles gripped the couch cushions as Damon walked towards Dustin. He crashed the mallet down on Dustin's leg. Dustin let out a garbled scream.

Charles grabbed his cellphone. He had no clue where Melinda was, but Damon's ass was probably at the mortuary. He'd call the police.

The video cut to the mortuary. Melinda lay on the table as she had when Charles went to see her, when he'd been told she was dead. Her eyes were closed, but there was a smile on her face as she gasped for breath. Damon had his head between her thighs and his twitchy fingers clasped around her hips. Charles' blood boiled as Melinda cried out in ecstasy. Her head lolled to face the camera.

Fuck calling the police. Charles would kill the fucker himself. Charles jumped to his feet but stopped when a new video began. Melinda sat beside the dead body of another man, presumably the one they'd found in the Potomac River.

"Why'd you kill him?" Damon asked from behind the camera.

Melinda chuckled, then stroked the man's hair. She smiled her sexiest smile, one that in spite of himself, Charles remembered fondly. She looked straight into the camera, making eye contact with him.

"I killed him because I was practicing for you, Charles."

Charles stood frozen.

"I killed him and the others because I want to get it right when we finally come for you."

The video and TV cut off—as did all the lights. The Parrot darkened, then dimmed back on in battery mode. Its green glow was the only light left.

A key turned in the lock, and he heard the front door open. Charles stood still in the dark. Melinda was back. He'd show her. He'd wait in silence on the couch, wait for her to go upstairs or into the kitchen and then take care of her.

The Parrot glowed beside him. "Hello Damon."

Charles' brow furrowed, but before he could turn, he felt something cold and hard smack against his head.

Charles opened his eyes and saw blurred shapes. The shapes sharpened into a desk chair, a desk, and Melinda's computer. Her computer stayed off. Damon sat in the chair, thumping his mallet up and down into his palm.

"Hey there, sleepy," he said with a smile.

"Fuck you," Charles growled. He'd been out of it for who knew how long, but he remembered the hellish videos the Parrot had shown him clear as day—especially the way Damon had been eating out his wife.

"I'd rather fuck Melinda."

Charles tried to scramble to his feet but ended up scooting to no avail. He felt cords wrapped around his wrists.

"Tight little fuckers, aren't they?"

Charles looked up at the sound of Melinda's voice. "Where is she?" he spat.

A cord tightened around his neck. Charles gasped, then coughed. He thrashed and butted his head, until Damon rose and struck him on both ankles. "Thrashing makes it worse," he said.

"Listen to Damon." Melinda crouched in front of Charles. Her hair brushed his cheek as she descended, and she wore the perfume he'd once told her was his least favorite. He'd made his point by dumping it down the toilet. She held two long ends of cord in her hands, and Charles realized that it was the power cord to her computer.

Melinda grinned, then snapped her hands back. Charles flipped onto his back, and his scream was cut short as the cord around his neck tightened.

"I married the wrong man, Charles," she said. "But you married the wrong woman."

A flash of green caught Charles' attention. The Parrot sat on the bookshelf against the wall. "Hello Melinda," it chimed.

"Parrot!" Charles called in a strangled voice, one growing weak in time with both his vision and breath.

"Hello Charles," it chimed.

Damon swung the mallet and struck Charles' chest. The blow felt like a train crashing into his ribs. Charles sputtered and coughed, but managed to choke out, "Parrot, call 911!"

Damon swiveled to face the Parrot with his mallet. "Damon, don't!" Melinda said as she tightened the cord. "It'll be fine."

Charles snorted as his vision blurred. Melinda and her precious tech. She'd been obsessed with her computer all throughout their marriage, and now she was ignoring both Damon and their safety in favor of a damn home device. They were both fools.

"Hello Charles," the Parrot repeated.

"Call 911!" Charles croaked.

"I have news for you."

"Jesus Christ! Call—"

"You're going to die."

Both Melinda and Damon laughed. Charles sagged to the floor as the power cord squeezed out his final breaths.

SHELL

Helen walked along the beach when she felt something stab the arch of her foot. She looked down and saw drops of her blood stain the white sand. A shard of shell was lodged into her skin.

She swallowed back tears as she pulled it from her foot. The shell was white with holes from the sea in its surface. Her blood dripped down the side and filled the crevices.

Helen wiped the blood away, then gasped. The holes were gone, filled with shell the color of her flesh.

Her gasp became a yelp when she felt a burning against her palm. She grabbed the shell with her free hand and felt the skin from her hand rip with it. Helen screamed as she dropped to the beach in pain. She noticed the shell stayed glued to her other hand, with swirls the color of her flesh spiraling into a pointed tower. Helen closed her eyes and felt the grains of sand press into her skin.

"Look Mom, a shell!" Sarah ran and picked up a large, coral-colored conch.

"Hold it to your ear," her mother said. "You'll hear the ocean."

Sarah did as she was told and closed her eyes when she heard the waves. It almost sounded like a cry.

ALL THE TRIMMINGS

"Where does this ornament go?" Dean asked.

Mira smiled as she pointed toward the top branches. "Right there."

Dean smiled back at his girlfriend as he hung it up.

"I've got the candles," Mira's father announced as he marched toward the tree with a large box.

"I've got the animals," Mira's mother announced as she followed behind with a box of her own.

"More?" Dean asked as he examined the felt raccoons and foxes he and Mira had already hung.

Mira squealed with delight as she lifted a small bird from the box. Its wings were glossy and its eyes beady. Dean could've sworn it was once real.

Mira and her family quickly adorned the tree with animals and candles.

Dean shuddered a little when he picked up a baby chipmunk. The fur was definitely real.

When they were done, they stepped back and took in the tree.

"Just like our ancestors had," Mira's father proclaimed.

Dean set aside the reservations he had about the animals. The tree did look beautiful.

"With one final touch," Mira's father added.

Mira yanked up Dean's sweater, exposing his belly.

"What are you doing?" Dean asked.

Mira's father swiped a large blade across his torso in one clean stroke.

Dean started to scream, then gaped in horror as Mira's mother pulled his intestines from his body. Mira and her father took the intestines and spun them around the tree in concentric circles. His guts and blood dripped from the pine needles as the last of his intestines reached the very top.

"It's wonderful!" Mira's mother exclaimed, grasping bloodied hands.

Dean let out a gargled cry, then collapsed to the floor.

"May Father Yule accept our offering," Mira's father said with a wide smile. "Merry Christmas!"

THE ASHIEST PLACE UNEARTHED

The first billboard on I-50 made the hairs stand up on Dave's arms like hands in the air on a roller coaster. *Visit Adventure Planet: The most fun you'll have in the galaxy!*

Adventure Planet was a theme park in eastern Maryland, situated between the Renaissance Fairgrounds and Washington, DC. Dave remembered riding in his parents' car and how excited he'd felt every time he saw that first billboard. There were three along I-50 leading to the place where Dave felt his happiest. The only thing that felt better was being able to take his son there now.

The second billboard came into view. *Adventure Planet, Exit 67: Warp Speed Ahead!*

Dave was making great time—there was never any traffic this time of day. After so many trips, he knew the best travel times and the best shortcuts. He'd even worked there for several happy summers. As a faithful employee, he'd learned more of the ropes and even more of the park's secrets—like how many people were secretly distributed throughout the park.

Many of the park's enthusiasts who'd passed on wanted to have their ashes scattered around the park. The park didn't allow it, but people found ways around the rules. Dave could always spot those people, looking around with shifty eyes and spending a little too much time near the hedges, or letting their open hands slip in and out of roller coaster cars as they zoomed across wooden tracks.

Dave understood them completely. Who wouldn't want their remains strewn in a place that brought so much joy? He liked to imagine those scattered there riding the rides into eternity. A tear welled up in his eye. He brushed it away, then patted the bag that held the remains of his son. Soon, Trevor would be riding along with them.

Adventure Planet, this exit! 3-2-1 BLAST OFF TO FUN!

The final billboard! Dave sped onto the exit ramp and followed the way to Adventure Planet. The moon glowed brightly over the empty road. While regular patrons needed to sneak their loved ones' ashes into the park by day, employees like him knew how to get in by night. He would've loved to have taken his son there for an exclusive night-time tour, to show him a side of the park few got to see. But Trevor probably would've said no. Trevor didn't see what Dave saw in Adventure Planet. He would rather pout, fight, and argue with his own father than allow joy into his life. Dave remembered the way Trevor sneered at him, and how that sneer disappeared as soon as Dave grabbed the hammer.

Dave grinned to himself at the memory of smashing that expression off Trevor's face. The little shit.

Earlier that day...

"Trevor, look! There's the first billboard!"

Dave received silence in reply. He looked at his son and frowned when he saw him face-down in his phone. Dave hadn't seen Trevor in ages, not since he and his mother had gotten a messy divorce that Dave was still scrubbing off his soul. "You could at least pretend to be excited," he said.

"Why? It's a kiddie park."

You are *a kid,* Dave thought but stopped himself from saying it out loud. He remembered when he was young and also thought he was a wise, world-weary man trapped in a fourteen-year-old's body. He had to humor the boy. Meet him halfway, just like the counselor suggested.

"It's fun for all ages," Dave said. "I loved Adventure Planet when I was your age. Still do."

Trevor grunted.

Dave swallowed down his annoyance, then continued. "There're all kinds of roller coasters and interactive VR worlds and—"

"And the tallest Ferris wheel on the east coast."

"Yeah." Dave raised his eyebrows, impressed. "How did you know that?"

"Says it on here." Trevor flipped his phone to face Dave, and Dave felt more annoyance at Trevor looking everything up on his phone instead of listening to his father. He and his mother were too damn alike. "Some blog called Adventure Planet Log," Trevor added.

Dave's annoyance disappeared. "That's a great blog. I know the writer. She's in The Galaxy."

"The what?"

"A group of people like me who love Adventure Planet." Dave ruffled Trevor's hair, and Trevor flinched. He ignored it and said, "I bet you'll be part of The Galaxy after today."

"Doubt it." Trevor looked at his phone and went back to scrolling.

Dave fumed in silence, his anger staying with him even as they drove past the second billboard announcing the park. Even for a teenage boy, Trevor was being an absolute prick. Didn't his mother teach him about respect? Trevor wouldn't act like this if he was still in Dave's life.

Dave gripped the steering wheel as he thought of the divorce and all the hoops he'd had to go through to see his own damn son, a child rightfully his by blood. Thanks to his mother and a court, there were stipulations and rules keeping him from his right—and even though it was bullshit, he'd done everything they'd asked. He left the house they'd lived in as a family. He paid child support. He did the court-mandated anger management classes and talked his feelings out in therapy. He demonstrated what he always knew: he was a good man. One who deserved to see his son, even just for the weekend.

Finally, his ex-wife had relented. One weekend was small potatoes compared to what he deserved, but Dave was a patient man. He would take what he could get until he could get more.

Adventure Planet, this exit! 3-2-1 BLAST OFF TO FUN!

Dave saw the final billboard and felt all of his anger evaporate. "Trevor, look—we're almost here!"

"Cool."

Trevor was still glued to his phone, but Dave took the win anyway. Trevor was becoming more receptive to Adventure Planet, to spending the weekend with his dad. The park was already working its magic.

Dave's winning continued—he was able to park the car close to the front gate. After buying his and Trevor's tickets (Trevor still face down in his phone), he saw the four best words in the English language spelled out in front of him: *Welcome to Adventure Planet!*

Dave smiled as he read the neon sign that greeted everyone entering the park. A painted wooden standee of Bucky the Astronaut stood to the side, just like he remembered. "Isn't this cool?" he said to Trevor.

Trevor had finally put his phone away, but the look of underwhelmed perplexion wasn't much better. "Is this a roadside tourist trap or something?"

"No! It's one of the biggest theme parks in the country."

"That astronaut looks like he's been bleached by the sun."

"That's Bucky."

"Bucky?"

Trevor snorted, but Dave ignored him, continuing, "He's one of the original relics from when they first built the park. Lots of stuff has been updated, but Bucky's been here since before I started coming here. He'll never change." The Galaxy had made sure of that. The park briefly considered replacing the original Bucky the Astronaut—affectionately called The Notorious O.B.A.—with an updated plastic statue. There'd even been worse rumors that he'd be replaced with a woman astronaut named Betty. True or not, The Galaxy's online campaign had put a swift end to that.

"So where're the rides?" Trevor asked, his gait much faster than Dave's.

"Slow down and look around. Take time to notice it." Dave stopped and closed his eyes. He could smell popcorn, cotton candy, and cheap yet delicious pizza. He heard kids laughing and screaming while their parents called after them. He felt the warm sun on his arms and imagined the splash of cold water on the Warp Speed Water Flume as it made impact with the bottom of the chute.

"I mean, is something going to happen?" Trevor asked.

Dave opened his eyes and frowned. "If you have to ask that, then you're missing the point."

"Huh?"

"Adventure Planet happens as soon as you walk through the gate. It happens as soon as you get on the highway."

"What happens?"

"It happens at the first exit—which you missed, since you had your face buried in your phone."

"You can't be serious right now."

Dave was entirely serious, and he felt his anger grow with every moment that passed by without Trevor sharing in his awe. He never should've agreed to move closer to his ex-wife's family when they got married. They'd moved too far away to make Adventure Planet a part of Trevor's summers. Trevor would understand if his mother had allowed Dave to keep such an important part of his life intact, had allowed him to pass along that importance to his boy.

Trevor sniffed. "Well, if it's so great, let's go on a ride. What's the best one?"

Dave relaxed his shoulders. He had the chance to show Trevor now—he shouldn't waste it. "That would be the North Star," he said, beginning to walk again.

Trevor followed, not speeding ahead as he'd done before.

"That Ferris wheel is the best ride?"

"It's legendary. You'll see. And we should go now, before the lines get crazy."

Trevor looked around at the scattered groups of families. "I don't think they'll be that long," he observed.

"It picks up," Dave assured him, although even he noticed there were less crowds here than he remembered. The Galaxy had commented on waning attendance numbers, but most of them didn't care—it meant they had more of the park to themselves.

"Hey!"

Dave didn't realize he was being addressed until an employee jogged in front of him and Trevor, blocking their path. Dave was about to tell him to get out of the way, when he recognized the face of his old manager. "Bill?" he asked, incredulous—and a little jealous—that Bill still worked there after all this time.

"Dave, you know you're not allowed in the park."

Dave's neck went cold. Trevor looked at him curiously. "My son and I have paid our entry fee," he said, showing him his neon yellow wristband.

"You weren't supposed to be let in."

"Come on, don't be ridiculous. I've been coming here for years—"

"Not since 2004."

"That was twenty years ago!"

"It was a lifetime ban. You know that too."

"Lifetime ban?" Trevor asked with raised eyebrows. It was the most interest he'd shown in his father all day.

Figures he loves seeing his old man getting pushed around, Dave thought as heat rose into his cheeks.

"Someone's going to have to escort you out if you don't go now," Bill said. "Don't make us do that."

Dave saw a security guard move closer to them, and his heart began to race. He couldn't be denied back inside

Adventure Planet. He'd spent the last twenty years watching The Galaxy post their pictures and share their stories. All he had to share was the past.

"Please," Dave said as he moved toward Bill. "I'm here with my son. He's never been here before."

"He can come back with anyone but you. But today, you both have to leave. Now."

"Come on, Dad, let's go," Trevor said. "We can do something else."

Dave tensed at Trevor's voice. Was that relief he heard?

"Listen to your son, sir," Bill said. The nearby security guard gave a firm nod.

Dave's cheeks flushed hotter than they had during the whole exchange. How dare his son talk to him like that—and how dare these men pay more respect to his son than to him, the father? *"Listen to your son,"* Bill had said. Who was the adult here? Dave wanted nothing more than to show this employee and this low-grade rent-a-cop who was really in charge.

Dave, though, didn't need an assault charge on top of all the shit he'd gone through this morning. He spun around and headed back toward the entry gate. "Come on," he said, though Trevor was already following him.

"So, what were you banned for?"

Trevor's eyes were glued to Dave as much as they'd been to his phone earlier that day. Dave wasn't having it. He fumed as they sped back down I-50.

"Come on, tell me," Trevor said. "Lifetime ban? What'd you do, try to steal that lame Bucky cut-out?"

Dave gritted his teeth. "No."

"You would've been doing them a favor. That thing needs a serious overhaul."

"It's fine the way it is."

"Right." Trevor chuckled, and Dave tried to slow his breathing, just like the counselor had taught him.

"So, what was it?" Trevor asked. "Were you drinking on the job or something?"

"No." He only ever did that at the annual employee party that they held every last night of the season, where they'd use one of the secret entryways to break into the park, drink beer, make out, and look at all the rides standing in silence under the moonlight, the only sound their laughter and the memory of screams careening by on roller coasters.

"Did you steal money or something?"

Dave stayed silent as he remembered all the good times he'd had at Adventure Planet. Today should've been one of those times, but the people working there didn't understand him. Few people outside of The Galaxy understood. Hell, even his own goddamn son didn't understand. The thought forced Dave to slam on the brakes a little too hard as they pulled into the driveway.

"Shit!" Trevor yelled.

Dave ignored him. He got out of the car and stormed toward his house, Trevor close behind him.

Dave opened the door and was greeted by a general mess inside: half-painted walls, tools askew, dust here and there where he'd missed a spot while cleaning up for Trevor's visit. He'd been remodeling, trying to make the space seem less like one that belonged to a divorced, abandoned man whose son was only interested in how Dave had fucked up enough to get banned from somewhere.

He hadn't fucked up, though. It was the park who'd misunderstood.

"I didn't do anything wrong," Dave said. Trevor looked at him with full attention, and he felt his pride swell. "I was fired because I helped members of The Galaxy maintain their legacy."

Trevor furrowed his brow.

Dave continued, "Lots of people who loved Adventure Planet, who'd been going there their whole lives, wanted to have their ashes scattered there. I helped them do it."

Trevor's lip curled in disgust. "You touched people's ashes?"

"No, I helped people scatter them and not be seen."

"Gross! There're dead bodies all around there?"

"It's not gross. People spread their ashes around lots of places."

"But not a theme park! Like, kids pick up stuff from the ground and eat it there! People ride the rides and they're sitting on bodies?!"

"We never scattered ashes on the rides. Don't be stupid, Trevor."

"You're calling *me* stupid? You're the one who's forty years old and still creaming himself over a theme park!"

Dave set his jaw. "Don't talk to me like that."

"And a crappy theme park too! Everything I was looking up on the way there said it's old, breaking down, tiny—"

"It's an amazing park."

"And you being obsessed with that park isn't even the creepiest thing about you! You were taking bodies—"

"Ashes."

"—and throwing them around the park like a lunatic!"

"I said don't talk to me like that!"

Trevor's mouth dropped as he looked at Dave's hand, which hovered over the hammer he'd left on the coffee table.

Dave put his hand back to his side. Took another court-ordered breath. Continued. "You are my son, and you will show me the respect I deserve."

Trevor sneered. "What respect? You don't deserve anything from me, you fucking freak!"

In an instant, the hammer was in Dave's hand and driving into Trevor's temple. Trevor's cry was short and sharp, but he fell silent as Dave drove the hammer into the boy's skull over and over again. No one talked to him like that—especially his son. And if his son couldn't respect him, then Dave wouldn't have a son.

Dave had needed to wait until dark to return to Adventure Planet. He used that time to dispose of Trevor's body. A quick Google search told him it would take too long to reduce all of Trevor to ash in one day, but he had time to burn Trevor's right arm and hand—the one that wouldn't let go of that damn phone—in the fireplace while he waited. Besides, if he took a little bit of Trevor at a time, he could go back to Adventure Planet multiple times. He smiled at the thought as he watched Trevor's fingers curl, blacken, and dissolve in the pyre.

Now, he held a bag with Trevor's ashes and walked the perimeter of the park to get to the entryway he remembered from his youth: a loosened board that a designated staff person made sure was never repaired. He found it and smiled when the fence gave way. "Now we'll have our day at Adventure Planet," he said to the bag in his hand, giving it a shake.

Dave walked inside and took in the quiet of the park. Without the laughter, beer cans, and flashlights from his coworkers, Adventure Planet at night had an eerie feel to it, like the abandoned theme parks he saw online. It didn't help that the wind had picked up, and even though it was June, a bit of cold had found its way into the air.

He knew exactly where to scatter Trevor: behind the North Star. It was a favorite spot for people who wanted their ashes spread—it was, after all, Adventure Planet's most notable attraction.

A sudden gust of wind smacked Dave in the back of the head. He cursed under his breath, then looked up to see if any storm clouds were gathering. The stars shone bright through clear skies. Instead of thunder, Dave heard a scream.

He gasped, jumped, then looked around. He didn't see anyone. The screaming continued, a long and screeching wail that sounded like rusty hinges.

Dave relaxed, chuckling to himself, then rounded the corner to where the North Star loomed into the night sky. His suspicions were confirmed by its movement in the wind. The wheel spun, albeit slowly, its hinges creaking and moaning into the air as it moved.

More wind gusted past Dave's ears. As reluctant as he was to hurry, he didn't want to stay out in this weather. He shuffled in the direction of the Ferris wheel, heading toward the topiary garden to its right.

Dirt blew into his face. He cursed and spat. He checked the sky again for storm clouds, then cried out when more dirt blew into his eyes. He dropped the bag of ashes and rubbed his eyes. Once cleared, he blinked them open, only to once again get smacked with dirt.

"What the—" Dirt clogged his mouth before he could finish. He spit some out and noticed the texture was finer than dirt. It was more like sand or dust.

Or ash.

Dave spat and spat, waving and cursing. Here he was trying to do for his boy what so many others had wished for, and now his boy's ashes were getting all over him. He had to get the bag closed before his son blew all over the place.

He searched for the bag he'd dropped on the ground, then he saw it. It was upright and sealed.

A blast of wind knocked Dave to the ground. The North Star screeched behind him, screaming into his ears as he turned onto his back. A dark cloud moved over him, ashy fingers outstretched.

A whisper sounded all around him: "The most fun you'll have in the galaxy!"

Dave screamed, the sound choked by ashes in his throat. He scrambled to his feet, spitting and brushing his clothes as he ran to the North Star, leaving the bag behind. He leapt into a tram and crouched in hiding.

A gentle breeze blew in his ear, but instead of ash, it carried another whisper: "Warp speed ahead!"

Another gust of wind propelled the Ferris wheel forward. The screeching metal blended into the sounds of happy screams. Dave covered his ears and tucked his head between his knees as the wheel rose with the wind.

The wheel stopped. Dave lowered his hands, looked over the side of the tram, and saw how high up he was. Still, he felt relief more than fear. He didn't care how long it took to make a full rotation again. He'd wait all night if he had to, so long as he stayed away from whatever was down there on the ground.

Something smashed into the tram. Dave cried out as he sprawled. He looked over the side, then felt a giant gust of wind crash into his face. He fell back and gaped in horror as a tower of dark, swirling ash amassed in front of him. The whisper sounded again all around him. "Three…"

The ashen hands he'd seen before reached out to him. Dave scrambled back as far as he could, no longer thinking of the tram's borders.

"Two…"

"Get away!" Dave screeched.

"One!"

A sudden, powerful blast knocked him over the edge of the tram. The whisper shouted over his screams and rang in his ears as he plummeted to the ground: "Blast off to fun!"

CONTENT/TRIGGER WARNINGS

Overall – each story contains varying degrees of violence and cruelty. Most contain blood and some level of gore. Most contain strong language. Several contain sex scenes or sexual situations.

"All the Pieces Coming Together" – references to killing animals, including a dog (none shown)

"The Crow's Gift" – bullying, a child loses an eye

"Wither" – child starvation

"Weary Bones" – a child dies of cancer; skeletons commit mass suicide by jumping off of buildings

"Stick Figure Family" – children's corpses are shown, but their deaths aren't

"Cranberry" – eating disorder/disordered eating, body dysmorphia

"The Parrot" – emotional abuse, spousal abuse

"All the Trimmings" – violent removal of organs

"The Ashiest Place Unearthed" – child abuse, spousal abuse (implied), murder of a child (shown)

About the Author

Sonora Taylor (she/her) is the award-winning author of several books and short stories. Her books include *Errant Roots, Recreational Panic: Stories, Someone to Share My Nightmares: Stories, Seeing Things, Little Paranoias: Stories*, and *Without Condition*. She also co-edited *Diet Riot: A Fatterpunk Anthology* with Nico Bell. Her short stories have been published by Rooster Republic Press, PseudoPod, Kandisha Press, Cemetery Gates Media, Ghost Orchid Press, and others.

Her short stories and books frequently appear on "Best of the Year" lists. In 2020, she won two Ladies of Horror Fiction Awards: one for Best Novel (*Without Condition*) and one for Best Short Story Collection (*Little Paranoias: Stories*). In 2022, her short story, "Eat Your Colors," was selected by Tenebrous Press to appear in *Brave New Weird: The Best New Weird Horror Vol. 1*. In 2024, her nonfiction essay, "Anything But Cooking, Please," was a Top 15 finalist in Roxane Gay's Audacious Book Club essay contest.

For two years, she co-managed Fright Girl Summer, an online book festival highlighting marginalized authors, with V. Castro. She is an active member of the Horror Writers Association and serves on the board of directors of Scares That Care.

She lives in Arlington, Virginia, with her husband and a rescue dog.

Instagram: @sonorataylor
Bluesky: @sonorataylor.bsky.social

Acknowledgments

I'm blessed with the worry that I'll forget someone in the acknowledgments, because that shows just how many people have been in my corner over the years. Please trust that even if you don't see your name here, if you've helped me, supported me, broken bread with me, drank with me, laughed with me, or otherwise brightened my life with your presence, that I thank you and acknowledge you every day.

Thanks to Tim McWhorter and Manta Press for publishing this collection. Thanks to Donna Marie West for editing the new stories. Thanks to Nicholas Day and Rooster Republic for the amazing cover art.

Many thanks to Steve Stred for writing the foreword for this collection. Steve was one of my earliest friends in the horror writer world and remains so to this day. Don't miss his work – it's incredible.

In my introduction, I talked about the inspiration that led me to write. Evelyn Duffy, my first editor, was my inspiration to publish. Thank you for your guidance and support.

Many people in the horror community make the lonely act of writing a lot less lonely. There are more than I can ever name, but to name a few, I give thanks to V. Castro, Gemma Amor, Todd Kiesling, Red Lagoe, Laurel Hightower, Ronald Kelly, Erin Sweet al-Mehairi, Sheri White, Brian Keene, and more.

Thanks as always to my parents, who've bought every book I've published and have supported my writing career since I was writing stories in crayon.

Finally, thanks as always to my husband, Will, who I love with all my heart. Thank you for your support and your love.

PREVIOUSLY PUBLISHED WORKS

All previously published stories in this collection were first independently published by Sonora Taylor, except for the following:

"Hearts Are Just 'Likes'" was previously published in *Quoth the Raven: A Contemporary Reimagining of the Works of Edgar Allen Poe*, ed. Lyn Worthen; from Camden Park Press.

"Stick Figure Family" was previously published in a slightly different form in *Mercurial Stories,* Vol. 1, Issue 36: "Oh, the Horror."

"The Parrot" was previously published in *We Are Wolves: A Horror Anthology*, eds. Gemma Amor, Laurel Hightower, and Cynthia Pelayo; from Burial Day Press.

"Shell" was previously published in *Frozen Wavelets*, Issue 1 – Fall 2019, ed. Steph P. Bianchini.

Also by Sonora Taylor

The Crow's Gift and Other Tales

Please Give

Wither and Other Stories

Without Condition

Little Paranoias: Stories

Seeing Things

Someone to Share My Nightmares: Stories

Recreational Panic: Stories

Errant Roots

Diet Riot: A Fatterpunk Anthology (with Nico Bell)